EDGE: THE BIGGEST BOUNTY

AUTHOR'S NOTE

The greater part of this book is devoted to the story of Edge (then Captain Josiah C. Hedges) during the War Between The States. Although complete in itself, enjoyment may be enhanced by first reading *Killer's Breed*, *The Blue, The Grey And The Red*, *Seven Out of Hell*, and *Vengeance is Black*.

Edge: The Biggest Bounty

GEORGE G. GILMAN

NEW ENGLISH LIBRARY
TIMES MIRROR

for J.O'L
who invited me to Stratford –
the one out west, naturally

An N E L Original 1974
© George G. Gilman, 1974

*

FIRST N E L PAPERBACK EDITION MARCH 1974
REPRINTED MARCH 1974

*

N E L Books are published by The New English Library Limited from Barnard's Inn, Holborn, London E.C.1. Made and printed in Great Britain by C. Nicholls & Company Ltd.

45001789 3

CHAPTER ONE

The stream ran fast and clear through the grassy foothills east of the Big Horn Mountains in the far north of Wyoming Territory. To a man with a romantic view of the world, the stream's frenetic progress might have indicated a natural anxiety to seek out a broader water course towards the Missouri and thus gain eventual freedom in the vast, unbanked void of the ocean. The bright mid-morning sunlight which dropped from a cloudless sky, causing the surface of the stream to shimmer and the rock-tossed spume to sparkle, might have encouraged such an impression of something vitally alive and flexing its strength in an attempt to shake loose of restraining fetters.

The tall man riding the grey gelding saw the stream as a means to refresh himself and his mount on his long journey beneath the energy-draining harshness of the sun. For he was the man called Edge and it had been many years since he had taken a romantic view of anything.

He checked his horse to a reluctant walk as he rode down the long slope of a meadow towards the stream. Then, at the low bank, he dismounted and allowed the animal to drink first. As the horse sucked greedily from the strong flow, the man made a careful surveillance of the terrain to the south, west and north. He knew the east to be empty. And he doubted if there was any imminent threat from the other directions. But he had learned the hard way that vigilance was the first essential for survival in a world where romance was for the very young or the very old and the harsh reality of death struck at everyone eventually. And he had seen many men – and women – who had failed to abide by this prerequisite, spilling their life blood as they learned the lesson too late.

Some might feel that such people were life's winners if one of the options of alertness was the risk of becoming like Edge.

He was a tall man, standing three inches over six feet and deceptively lean: for he weighed close to two hundred pounds. Not an ounce of this was excess fat and where his tight-fitting black denim shirt and dark blue levis contoured his torso, arms and thighs the outline was of knotted muscles rather than smooth, padded flesh. His face warned that he had not developed such a powerful strength for the simple pleasure of mere achievement.

It was a thin face, stained a dark brown by his heritage and deeply lined by the vagaries of weather and the harshness of the kind of life fate had mapped out for him. From the dark ground of his face, his narrow eyes looked upon the world as if they were chips of ice, bright blue and chillingly cold. His cheekbones were high, flanking a hawklike nose. His mouth was thin, cruelly so at times, above a firm jawline which seemed to offer a constant challenge. The whole was framed by thick, jet-black hair which dropped from beneath the wide brim of a low-crowned hat to brush his shoulders. Some of his features had been inherited from a Scandinavian mother. Most had been drawn from his Mexican father. Grief and hatred, deprivation and violence had moulded the basic structure into a form which was at once attractive and ugly, dependent upon the mood of the man or the eye of the beholder.

As the slitted eyes surveyed the rolling grassland of the low valley and the rocky ridges of the mountains beyond, Edge looked his meanest. His cheeks and jaw were heavily stubbled and the lids enclosing the penetrating blueness of his eyes were red from almost continuous searching and lack of sleep. And the Mexican hawkishness of his features was emphasised by a thinning down of the flesh caused by many days of fast. As he stretched out full-length on the lush bank and saw his reflection in the broken surface of the stream, he thought he had not looked so emaciated as this since he was a Union prisoner in the Confederate hellhole of Andersonville.* That had been many years ago, during the War Between the States which had taught him

* See: *Edge: The Blue ,The Grey And The Red.*

6

so many lessons about survival. In the interval, there had been few prolonged periods when he had not found it necessary to recall those evil teachings.

He drank his fill and as he straightened he felt the chillness of the water inside him do a little to combat the fatigue which had been threatening to overtake him all morning and throughout most of the preceding night. But he knew he would have to rest soon, and he thought that he would now be able to do so without waking after a few minutes to escape the nightmare. He didn't know how many days he had ridden, halting only to rest the gelding, or how many miles he had covered. But the Dakotas were far behind him, perhaps still suffering the turmoil of Sioux on the warpath or perhaps not. It didn't matter for Indians were of no concern to him, except that their proximity made it more essential than ever to stay alert. In Wyoming it wasn't the Sioux, of course. But the Arapaho, Shoshone, Crow and Cheyenne tribes might be stirred up. Alternatively, a hunting party of any tribe might see a lone white rider as an easy kill.

Edge filled his canteen and swung into the saddle, his eyes raking the stream in both directions and spotting a point where it looked easiest to ford. The gelding was army-trained and courageous. Edge was an expert rider and had quickly developed an understanding with his unfamiliar mount. The horse appreciated this and had soon learned to trust the man. Thus, when Edge heeled him forward into the rushing, ice-cold water, the gelding did not hesitate. Sure-footed on the water-smoothed rocks of the stream bed, the animal picked his way carefully across and, clear on the far side, responded readily to the demand for a canter up the western slope of the valley.

At the top there was a trail, running south-east to north-west. It looked to be quite well used, rutted by wagon wheels and marked by shod hooves. For no other reason than it kept the sun at his back instead of glaring into his eyes, Edge heeled his mount in the north-westerly direction. The deserted line shack crouched at the centre of a cottonwood grove a mile or so up the trail. Its windows were hung with cobwebs instead of glass and the roof of the stoop had collapsed. The corral fence had rotted. A wooden sign canted drunkenly on leaning posts, the lettering faded and barely legible: WYOMING–MONTANA–COLO-RADO LINE. Painted across this, more recently and less expertly, was the legend: *This line might be finished, but we ain't (signed) Messrs. Wells & Fargo.*

Edge sidled his horse in closer to the broken sign, to read the message scrawled on a square of card nailed to one of the supporting posts: *Sam Lynch's Birthday Celebration. This Sunday after church. Come one, come all. Warm welcome to friends and strangers. Jerusalem. Three miles thataway.*

The arrow pointed the way Edge had been heading and he pondered the implications of the sign for a full minute. It wasn't the fact of the celebration which concerned him: he didn't know what day it was or whether the Sunday mentioned had gone or was yet to come. It was the prospect of riding into a town, and seeing people, which gave him pause for thought. He had stopped off in only one town on his long ride west, this visit occasioned by the need to buy fresh clothes, a handgun, shells for the Winchester resting in the saddle-boot, tobacco and food supplies. He had wasted little time in making the purchases and ridden out fast, veering away from the trail to ensure that he continued to suffer the bitter pangs of grief in isolation.

For this was the purpose of his long, geographically aimless ride – to put time and distance between himself and the mound of earth which marked the source of his torment, in the hope that the passage of the days and the passing of the miles would act as a salve to the deep hurt mixed with anger which Elizabeth's death had generated within him.* His self-imposed exile from his fellow-citizens served a dual purpose: by nature he was a loner and had no wish to put his grief on display, and also it was to protect others from a possible chain-reaction in violence if he found himself unable to conquer the sorrow.

This was a very real danger, for just as he had discovered a natural bent for being alone in a world where the herd instinct was strong, so too had he been faced with the inevitable truth that his instinctive reflex to being hurt was to retaliate with a harsher punishment: this in a world which, for the most part, frowned upon such rough, personal justice. That these charac-

* See: *Edge: Sioux Uprising.*

8

teristics had been born during a bloody war and nurtured in its even bloodier aftermath was no defence. And Edge made no attempt to defend himself – even to himself. He was the way he was and had learned to accept it. Others either accepted it, or paid the price of taking exception to it.

So Edge was protecting others, rather than himself, by staying clear of civilisation as he tried to lose the memory of his wife and the way she had died – in the shrouds of time and space. Twice before, people Edge had loved had died violently. But on those occasions there had been a clear-cut way to alleviate his grief. He had searched for, found and killed their murderers. First the men who had tortured and shot his brother Jamie.* Then the man who had burned to death Jeannie Fisher, the first woman after his mother he had loved.† But there was no such easy solution in the matter of Elizabeth's death for, without being aware of it at the time, Edge himself had caused her lingering agony. And with no specific target to lash out against, he was concerned that he might vent his frustration by killing the first innocent bystander who spoke out of turn or did the wrong thing. And although he had killed often, in a hundred different ways, and sunk to the level of a wild animal more times than he could count, he had always retained one final vestige of humanity. He had never caused suffering or death without good reason. And in the waking nightmare, crystallised in the bad dreams that kept sleep at bay, he was forced to face the fact that he alone bore the responsibility for his wife's death.

Should he, then, kill himself?

He gazed at the scrawled sign through narrowed eyes, but he was no longer seeing it. Abruptly, his lips curled back to show his very white, perfectly even teeth in a cold grin. The waking nightmare was over: and in the way of things, he knew sleep at last held out the promise of easy, refreshing rest. By his own code, he allowed every man one mistake. He had made his. This was the answer for which he had been searching over the days and the miles. And having found it, he unloaded his burden of guilt. The mistake and the death, along with the fantasies of

* See: *Edge: The Loner.*
† See: *Edge: Edge Out Of Hell*

9

what might have been, were placed firmly in the past where they belonged.

The future? He knew he needed sleep and his eyes swung to the sagging line shack behind the sign board. But he shook his head, for he was also certain that he could again mix among people without running the risk of blasting a hole in the first man to step on his toe. So he jerked on the reins to turn the gelding towards town, and the prospect of a featherbed, clean sheets and maybe even a tub of hot water.

The man who had measured the distance from line shack to town had had big ideas about the length of a mile. Edge, able to think logically again, judged he had ridden at least four miles when he met the girl – and there was not a trace of a settlement within sight. The trail had run parallel with the stream for a long way, then swung towards the west, passing through heavily wooded country. The terrain was undulating and the trail veered constantly to left and right, following the line of least resistance in terms of gradients. The woods were networked with many fast-running streams and the cool sound of the rushing water augmented the shade of the foliage overhead and made the discomfort of the morning ride a dim memory.

The girl with the gun was an ugly intrusion upon such a scene of pastoral peace. The girl without the gun would have been perfect. She was young, probably not yet twenty and her face was very beautiful. She had big, dark brown eyes which looked out nervously from a delicately sculptured face which showed no blemishes or paint and powder. It was framed by long, golden-coloured hair which tumbled from under her wide-brimmed bonnet in a cascade of waves to a point several inches lower than her shoulders. The bonnet was white, trimmed with blue. Her frothy dress picked up these colours and added dots of red in the form of buttons which began at the throat-high neckline and plunged between the thrusting swells of her breasts to finish at the nipped in waist. She was not riding her grey mare side-saddle and the skirt of the dress was puffed out on both sides of the horse, showing the hems of at least a dozen pink petticoats beneath.

The gun was a Henry repeating rifle which she held correctly, but uneasily. Edge guessed she knew about guns, but didn't like them.

Edge touched the brim of his hat. "Afternoon, miss," he greeted, reining his horse to a halt. "You going to shoot me?"

They had met at a point where the trail made an almost right-angled turn around the obstacle of a bluff. The babbling of the streams had prevented them hearing each other's approach and they saw each other simultaneously, over a distance of some twenty feet. Edge's Colt was in the tied-down holster at his right thigh, the Winchester was in the boot at the front and right of his saddle and the cut-throat razor nestled in the pouch at the back of his neck. The girl was riding with the Henry in her hand. It was only necessary to stop her horse and snap up the rifle to get the drop on Edge.

She struggled to drive the fear from her eyes. It was not successful, but her tone was strong and she jutted her delicate jaw to try to give an impression of hard determination. "Only if you make me. Please move out of the way."

Edge pursed his lips and surveyed her face and the generous curves and angles of her upper body – so blatantly displayed by the close-fit of the dress – with unconcealed admiration. Inwardly, he fought against making a comparison with Elizabeth. She too had pulled a gun on him within moments of their first meeting.* He drove the memories back into his deep subconscious.

"The *please* makes it hard to refuse, lady," he said, digging into his shirt pocket for the makings. He hooked a knee over the saddlehorn as he rolled the cigarette and ran his tongue along the gummed strip. His half smile and casual attitude heightened the girl's nervousness. "But I've got used to people stepping out of my way."

She sucked in a deep breath, but saw from his eyes what it did to her breasts and she expelled it in a rush. The rifle wavered, but not too far. "A gentleman would make way," she chided as he struck a match on the Winchester's stock and fired the cigarette.

* See: *Edge: Bloody Summer*.

The whiteness of the paper cylinder angling from the corner of his thin mouth seemed to emphasise the dark of many days' stubble and trail dirt covering his face. "Guess gentlemen went out when ladies started to tote guns," he replied easily.

Anger rose colour to her pale cheeks. "Do you expect me to ride through open country unarmed?" she demanded.

Edge blew smoke towards her but it disintegrated before it reached her. He dropped his leg, foot sliding into the stirrup. His lips parted in a full smile, but the meagre warmth that had been in his eyes was abruptly gone. "I expect you to point that rifle someplace else and to ride on by me, lady," he told her softly, his voice as cold as his eyes. "Trail's wide enough."

She swallowed hard, aware that the man's meanness was more than skin deep. She didn't dare release her grip on the rifle, even though she wanted to brush beads of perspiration from her forehead. "All right," she said suddenly. "I'll go to my left and you go to yours."

Edge nodded and sidled his horse from the centre of the trail. She did the same.

"But I'm keeping you covered the whole time, mister," she warned. "You bear that in mind."

Edge took the cigarette from between his teeth. His gaze was fixed upon the vibrant rise and fall of her young breasts. "I'm baring something else in mind right now,'" he muttered.

She made a throaty sound of disgust and clucked her horse forward. Edge held his gelding motionless at the foot of the rocky bluff.

"Watch out for the gopher hole," he snapped.

Alarm expanded her eyes as she dropped her gaze to the ground. Edge kicked free of his left stirrup and used the right as a purchase to power his leap across the width of the trail. He grasped the rifle barrel with both hands and dragged it to the side. The girl screamed and squeezed the trigger. The bullet burrowed into the hard-packed earth of the trail. Her horse reared at the explosion and she slid from the saddle, releasing the gun. Edge landed in a sure-footed crouch and caught her in his arms as he let the rifle drop.

"Please!" she gasped, staring up into his impassive face as she struggled to escape from his grip.

"Never say that to a man unless you first tell him what you're pleading for, lady," he advised, hooking his heel over the Henry's barrel before he set her down on her feet.

She was at once angry and terrified as she stood before the man, towering almost a foot taller than her. The mare snorted and scratched at the ground with a forehoof.

"What . . . what did you . . . you do that for?" she stammered, scared that she already knew the answer. Her wide eyes raked from his face, down to the rifle trapped beneath his foot, then up to the butt of the Colt sticking from his holster.

The cold grin cracked Edge's impassiveness. "Forget both ideas, lady," he told her softly. "The gun you wouldn't make. The other you might. And enjoyment ain't no punishment."

"Punishment?" she said, her voice shaky, "But I only – "

"You pointed a gun at me, lady," Edge rasped. "Nobody does that without paying some way."

She gulped. "What are you going to do?"

His discarded cigarette sent up a thin column of smoke from the ground, blue in the filtered sunlight. He moved his foot off the rifle to step on the smouldering tobacco. "How old are you?" he demanded.

She made no attempt to get closer to the Henry. "Nineteen next month," she replied in a whisper.

"Young enough," Edge said with a nod, and curled out an arm.

The girl screamed again. Edge dropped to one knee as his arm hooked around her neck and jerked her forward, then down. She fell, struggling, across the hard bar of his leg. The tone of her scream changed from fright to outrage as his free hand flipped up her skirt and petticoats and hooked over the waistband of her pantaloons. The almost sheer fabric of her underwear ripped with the ease of paper and seemed to shrivel to the sides, presenting the milky whiteness of her rear to full view.

"You – "

Edge's hard, copper brown hand slapped forcefully against the naked flesh and the girl gave a shriek of pain. "Never did me no harm," Edge shouted against the high-pitched sound screeching from her throat. His hand rose and fell in another spanking blow. "Course, I was younger than you when Pa gave my butt a whopping."

He hit her six times, making her flesh glow scarlet and reducing her screams to sobs. Then he rose, pushing her upright. Her face was highly-coloured with the rush of blood and anger. Tears of hurt coursed down it.

"You beast!" she flung at him.

He ignored her, stooping to pick up the Henry, then ejected its full load of shells. They glittered with an evil sheen as they flew through the sunlit air. He dropped the gun back on the ground and eyed the girl levelly as she massaged her pained rear end.

"You enjoyed that!" she accused.

He clicked his tongue against the roof of his mouth. "I won't say it hurt me more than it did you," he allowed, and turned to swing up into the saddle.

Her expression became scornful. "You're real brave, beating a girl!"

"It's easier than a man," he admitted. "But think about the whopping next time you reckon to point a gun at a stranger. The life you save could be your own."

He tapped the gelding's flanks with his heels and started on down the trail towards town. Once, he shot a glance over his shoulder, but the girl had made no move to pick up the Henry and reload it. She stood as he had left her, rubbing the source of her pain and staring after him vindictively.

"I hope I meet the man who pulls a gun on you and fires it, mister!" she yelled at him. "I'd sure like to shake his hand."

He grinned back at her. "Even for a lady as pretty as you, I don't reckon they'd dig him up just for that," he called in reply, and rode out of sight around a bend in the trail.

CHAPTER TWO

The marker board proclaimed: JERUSALEM – THE BEAT-
ING HEART OF THIS GREEN AND PLEASANT LAND.
(ELEVATION 4,000 FEET.)

Edge thought the surroundings looked green and pleasant
enough as he surveyed the undulating pasture spread out before
him. The trail dipped clear of the wooded hills and ran arrow
straight down a long slope and across a broad sweep of open
country. At the centre, it broadened between the facades of the
buildings which marked the one-street town, then narrowed
again and tapered in perspective towards the distant ridges of a
northern range of mountains. He counted eight farmsteads scattered across the broad, upland valley. Each was fenced, but
the better than five thousand head of cattle grazing on the lush
grass were free to roam over the entire range.

From a distance, the town did not seem to be beating with any
show of vitality, and as Edge rode closer the impression of lazy
tranquility became more marked. It was after midday now and
very hot out of the shade of the trees. There was not a breath of
a breeze. Smoke from cooking fires rose like solid columns of
grey and blue into the still air. But something – perhaps his own
imagination – wafted the appetizing aroma of food and coffee
under Edge's flared nostrils.

Nobody was in sight around the farmsteads, but an old man
slept in a rocker on the stoop before the barber's shop which was
the first building at the southern end of town. He woke at the
sound of the gelding's hooves and cracked his lips to show a
toothless smile.

"Howdy, stranger!" he said brightly, not getting up. "Come
for the celebration? Want a shave? Haircut?"

Edge halted his horse and gave the town a narrow-eyed once over. There was a church, two stores, a blacksmiths, a sheriff's office, a hotel incorporating a saloon and restaurant and a dozen houses. All were built of wood, only the St. David's Hotel reaching to double storey. Paint gleamed and windows shone. The signs over the business premises looked as fresh and clean as the day they were put up. The grass inside the picket fence surrounding the church was clipped short and the grave markers were scrubbed white. If anybody had raised dust from the street, it had been swept from the roofed sidewalks.

"How long's this town been here?" Edge answered with a question.

The barber chuckled and wiped an overflow of saliva from his chin. "Ten years, stranger," he said proudly. "Pretty good, uh? Looks like only yesterday, uh? Folks here like to keep things neat and tidy. Reason I figured you'd feel like a shave? Haircut?"

Edge scraped a hand over his stubbled jaw. "Shave, maybe. Later. Hair's okay."

He moved his horse forward, angling across the street towards the long length of hitching rail in front of the hotel.

"Sheriff Pitman, he don't like long-haired fellers, mister," the aged barber called. "He's got this theory about it and – "

"Could be the start of something big," Edge cut in wryly.

The old timer shrugged and resettled himself for another period of sleep as Edge dismounted and hitched his horse to the rail. A fat, middle-aged woman with a soured expression emerged from the dry goods store, carrying a loaded basket. She eyed Edge suspiciously as he slid the Winchester from the saddle boot and stepped up on to the sidewalk. He looked at her indifferently, prepared to exchange a greeting if she made the opening. She slowed her pace, and seemed to be waiting for something. Edge saw that the two storey building had three doorways – one at the centre for the hotel, a second for the restaurant and a third for the saloon. He licked his lips and tasted sweat and grit. He plumped for the saloon.

"Stay out of barrooms, young man!" the woman called stridently. "If you enter, the devil goes with you."

Edge halted with his hand on the batswings. His narrowed

eyes met her stare and captured it. "Ma'am, I don't give a shit," he drawled. "Just so long as he stands his round."

He pushed on into the dark interior to the sound of the woman's shocked gasp. The saloon was small, but big enough for a town the size of Jerusalem. And its furnishings and decorations matched the neat, clean lines of the town's exterior. The face of the handsome young bartender looked as polished as the rows of bottles and glasses arrayed in shelves behind him. Baskets of flowers hung from the ceiling emanated a mixture of sweet fragrances to mask the smell of alcohol – and perhaps, Edge thought, the odour of his travel-wearied body.

Three pairs of eyes followed him to the bar. Those of the bartender smiled a greeting. Two customers seated at a polished table – one young and beefy, the other in his forties and almost skeletonal – watched the newcomer with idle curiosity.

"Whiskey," Edge said, hooking a heel over the brass rail and leaning the Winchester against the bar front.

"Coming up," the bartender said brightly. "Here for the celebration?"

Edge watched as a shot glass was slapped on the bartop and a bottle was upended over it. Some of the liquor spilled. By the time he had raised the glass and thrown the drink against the back of his throat, a cloth had been produced and the spillage had been wiped off the wood.

"For the sleep," Edge said. "I figure I need twenty-four hours solid."

The bartender started to laugh. The glitter of the half-breed's eyes cut short his good humour. He gulped and blinked. "It's just that nobody sleeps in Jerusalem on Sam Lynch's birthday."

"I ain't nobody, and I don't know any Sam Lynch," Edge replied, reaching for the Winchester.

"Touch it and you're dead!" a voice warned curtly.

Edge froze, his eyes still locked on the nervous stare of the young bartender. The kid had to struggle, but finally he was able to look away, over the shoulder of his immobile customer.

"No trouble, sheriff," he blurted.

"You know my theory about guns and drink, Harvey," the

town's lawman replied flatly. "They don't mix. Turn around, mister. Slow, like you was in a jar of maple syrup."

"Or in a jam?" Edge countered easily as he complied with the order.

He leaned his back against the bar and hooked his thumbs over the buckle of his gunbelt as he surveyed the sheriff, and was subjected to a similar examination from the lawman. Pitman was pushing fifty and from his broad girth and nubile breasts which swelled his checked shirt that was about the only exercise he took. He was six feet tall and looked as if he might weigh in the region of two hundred and fifty pounds. His head was in proportion to his body, big boned and fleshy. The flat grey eyes seemed to be the the only points of hardness about him — discounting the Colt gripped in his pudgy right hand.

"It's one you made for yourself, feller," the lawman said. "That was my wife you insulted out on the street awhile back."

Edge showed no reaction. The other two customers switched their attention from the sheriff to Edge and back again. They seemed pleased that something was happening to enliven a dull day in a dull town.

The half-breed's silence irritated the lawman. "You got anything to say for yourself, mister?" he demanded.

"Yeah," Edge said, working saliva around in his mouth. "I'll say it to you and you can pass on the message to your wife. Keep your nose out of my business."

He spat on the spotlessly clean floor. Pitman gulped and Harvey gasped. The thin customer whistled softly. His friend leaned back in his chair, grinning.

"Oh, mister!" the sheriff breathed, swelling out his chest. "You're just a mess of trouble on two legs. Walking around looking for a place to happen."

"Kinda proves your theory about long hair, don't it?" Edge asked easily.

Pitman ignored the comment. "You got a choice," he rasped. "Get on your horse and ride out of Jerusalem. Or walk down to the gaol with me."

"You got a featherbed in the cell?"

"What do you think?" Pitman snarled, as angry at himself as

at Edge. For he knew he was facing a killer. Everything about the stranger stamped him as dangerous – the set of his features the fact that he toted a rifle when calling for a drink, the gun in the tied-down holster, and the apparent casual ease with which he faced the drawn Colt: only apparent because beneath the veneer of carelessness he was tensed and ready. His eyes gave that away. And from the cool look deep in back of the eyes, Pitman realised his bluff had been called with complete self-assurance. This man was no ordinary drifter with a big mouth and no guts.

"I think I'll ride out of town," Edge said softly, looking around the saloon and settling his indifferent gaze upon a poster nailed to a wall. It was a programme of events for the birthday celebrations, which he now knew to be forthcoming. One of the highspots was to be a prize fight between David Jefferson and Howy McNally.

"That's just fine," Pitman replied, visibly shaken by Edge's untroubled acceptance. "Pick up the rifle – one-handed by the barrel. And carry it that way."

The younger customer had replaced his grin with a sneer of contempt. His friend was as incredulous as the lawman. Edge picked up the gun in the manner described and levered himself away from the bar. Pitman moved to the side of the doorway, the Colt still trained on the half-breed's flat stomach.

"Forgot to pay for the drink," Edge said, coming to a halt halfway between the bar and the batswings.

"It's okay," Harvey replied to Edge's back. "Everyone's entitled to a free drink on Sam Lynch's birthday. Seeing as how you won't be in town tomorrow, you get yours today."

Edge gave a curt nod, then continued on towards the door, the Winchester trailing behind him, clutched by his left hand around the muzzle. The fat sheriff was to the left of him.

"Watch, Davy," the thin customer whispered to the well-built one.

"No sweat, sheriff," Edge said softly as he reached for the batswings with his free hand. "I'll ride out of town. . . ."

He went through the doors. The lawman moved into the gap behind him. Edge flicked his wrist and back heeled with his right foot. The stock of the Winchester crashed into one door. His boot hit the other. Both swung closed with terrific force. The Colt roared as the sheriff pushed it forward. But it was the lawman who screamed. Edge leaned far to the right, remaining on his feet and flipping over the rifle into both hands. The bullet from the revolver splintered wood from the front of a house across the street. People peered from windows and the more adventurous rushed from doorways. Pitman continued to scream as the Colt slipped from his helpless hand and clattered to the sidewalk. His hand hung limply through the narrow crack between the doors. The wrist had been fractured by the violent closure. Blood oozed from pulped flesh and dripped on to the sheriff's highly-polished toecaps sticking out from under the batswings. As Edge moved in front of the saloon entrance and looked in over the top of the doors into the contorted, stark white face of the lawman, the screams subsided into a low moaning.

". . . when I've caught up on lost sleep," the half-breed completed, shouldering the Winchester and digging into his hip pocket. He came up with a dollar bill, which he screwed up into a ball and flicked into the saloon. "For the drink, Harvey," he explained. "I'll collect on the free one tomorrow – if I'm up."

He turned away, heading for the hotel entrance and wondering why the name David Jefferson should trigger an indication of memory deep at the bottom of his mind.

A small man in a frock coat and carrying a carpetbag ran out of the hotel. "What happened?" he demanded anxiously. "Who's hurt?"

"Sheriff," Edge replied easily. "Somebody ought to get his arm out of the door before gangrene sets in. Pitman could wind up short-handed."

He shouldered by the shocked man and went into the hotel lobby.

CHAPTER THREE

David Jefferson was only the clue to the memory: not the memory itself. The name had to be reversed and one letter had to be altered. The answer came out Jefferson Davis, President of the Confederacy during the War Between the States.

It was mid-March in eighteen sixty-four, almost a month after the Federals had been defeated at Olustee, Florida and the Red River Campaign had been launched in an attempt to win Louisiana back into the Union. Far north of the major theatre of operations, Union Cavalry Captain Josiah C. Hedges led a train of four heavily-laden wagons through a lashing rain storm into a small town on the Tennessee-Virginia stateline. It was evening. The escort assigned to his command was comprised of six white troopers who had been with him from the start of the war* and eighteen Negroes. The latter were the survivors of a far larger group which had been freed from the yoke of Southern slavery by the white men with whom they now rode. All were garbed in Union blue, for the ex-slaves had been invited to enlist by General Ulysses S. Grant himself.

The entry into the tiny town of Hartford Gap on the south bank of the Clinch River marked the end of an uneasy ride for both the whites and the coloureds – and particularly for Hedges – even though there had been no trouble since the bloody skirmish with Quantrill's Raiders.† Major cause of friction between the men was the contempt in which the whites held the coloureds and the resentment with which this was met. For the release of the slaves had not been engineered for any altruistic or humanitarian motives. The whites – Sergeant Frank Forrest, Corporal

* See: *Edge: Killers Breed*
† Sec: *Edge: Vengeance is Black*

21

Hal Douglas and Troopers Billy Seward, Roger Bell, John Scott and Bob Rhett – never did anything freely with consideration for anybody but themselves. The slaves were needed so they were used. But, initially because of the coloureds' dogged stubbornness and latterly by dictate of military orders, the white troopers had been forced to accept the ex-slaves as comrades.

"You know something?" Bob Rhett said in his nasal New England accent that was pitched just high enough to hint at his homosexuality.

"I know a lot of things," Seward rasped. He had a baby face in which the eyes of a born-killer would have been incongruous had not the savagery of war twisted the mouth into a cruel line.

He viewed the huddle of buildings ahead with distaste, staring out from under the peak of his forage cap pulled low as an ineffective defence against the lashing rain. Rhett fingered the sopping wet pad of dressing covering a wound on the side of his head.

"I reckon it's right what they say about niggers being the missing link in the chain of man," the tall, thin fag said sourly. "I've never seen a man with so much body hair as the head boy of this bunch."

He was safe in voicing the word Hedges had banned for the Captain was blazing the trail out ahead while Rhett, Seward and Hal Douglas rode in drag positions.

"You been peeking again, Bob!" Douglas chided with a gaffuw. The corporal was probably the most incompetent non-com in the Union army. "Are they really black all over?"

Rhett scowled.

A rider loomed through the billowing curtain of wind-driven rain as the wagons and escort rumbled and clattered on to the muddy morass of Hartford Gap's main street. The fag swallowed hard as he recognised Manfred, the massive Negro who was only an enlisted man but looked upon by the other ex-slaves as their leader. Two other coloured troopers angled their mounts in to jog along beside Manfred. The expressions of all three were set in hard lines, their eyes wide and large as if impervious to the slanting rain.

Seward and Douglas slid hands under their water-run slickers and gripped the revolver butts protruding from unfastened holsters. The Negroes rode with both hands holding the reins.

"What a queer like you know about *man*kind?" the big black demanded.

Douglas attempted to pull his slight rank. "Get back to your positions, soldiers!" he snapped.

The blacks ignored him.

"You ain't no kinda man!"

"Billy!" Rhett cried. "Get him off my back."

Seward was about to jerk the Colt from the holster. Then he became aware of many pairs of eyes fixed upon him. He looked to left and right, finally over his shoulder. Since the wagons had moved out of open country into the confines of the street, the troopers covering the flanks and far rear had closed in. An arc of ten rain-bubbled black faces urged Seward to push the half-drawn gun back into the leather. He knew Hedges was far ahead, with Frank Forrest close by. And Bell and Scott were riding at point, equally unaware of what was happening.

"Hell, Bob, that ain't like you," the nervous youngster called, forcing lightness into his tone. "A man on your back is what makes you happy."

His laughter was strained. Nobody joined in.

"You stay away from my men," Manfred warned the quaking Rhett. "And you be careful what you call us." His thick lips folded back to show his very white teeth in a broad grin. "You say wrong thing again, I cut off your tongue. You try other thing, cut off something else."

Now the Negro troopers laughed, harsh and loud, as Manfred made the first move which led them all to fade back into the teeming rain.

"That guy's cracked!" Rhett spat out, not too loud in case the Negroes were within earshot.

"Sure, Bob," Douglas agreed with a snigger. "But I don't reckon you'll ever get to fill it in."

At the head of the short wagon train, Hedges heard the laughter through the hiss of rain and detected the mocking note in it. Someone was the butt of the sardonic humour and he guessed it was either himself or Rhett. He let it pass, seeing the courthouse a hundred yards down the street on the right, with the sodden Stars and Stripes fluttering valiantly from a pole over the porch to mark the building as the local command post. Two sentries flanking the doorway in the meagre cover of the porch confirmed that the military had taken over the building.

A small sigh of relief escaped his thin, compressed lips as he drew a hand across his narrowed eyes. The wind drove fresh drops into his face, as if anxious to launch one more attack before the man found dry shelter.

The rain had been the least of the young officer's worries on the long haul north from Chattanooga: and he had viewed it merely as a natural last straw attempting to break the back of his tenuous hold on command. The friction between the white men and the Negroes was of greater concern, but he thought he had that situation under as much control as was possible by gaining the respect of Manfred and Frank Forrest. The former gave it from gratitude and admiration; the latter out of grudging knowledge that Hedges was more capable of command and probably a faster, meaner and more savage killer than he was himself.

Time and again, as war transformed him from an educated farm boy into cool professional killer, Hedges had proved himself the best man to give the orders when the shooting started. Forrest had shown his appreciation of this fact by backing the officer. This was an accolade indeed from a man who in peacetime had been acknowledged as the toughest bounty-hunter in the south-west. Without exception, the other white troopers — who, like Hedges, had to learn the art of killing — gave their allegiance to Forrest: the man whose trade it was. So, only through the sergeant's grudging respect, was the officer able to keep the men in line and thus utilize their taste for violence and slaughter.

As Hedges raised an arm and the civilian drivers hauled on the reins of their teams to halt the wagons, Forrest moved up beside the Captain, his mean face cracked to show his crooked, tobacco-stained teeth in a grin. "Like I said at the start, Captain," he reminded. "This freight's too heavy for me."

24

Hedges quickly wiped the relief from his expression, but knew it was too late. The tall, broad-shouldered non-com had seen it and was enjoying the officer's discomfiture. The freight aboard the wagons, and what might possibly happen to it, had been the greatest cause of Hedges' anxiety on the gruelling trek across storm-lashed Tennessee. For it was composed of two million dollarsworth of gold confiscated from the Rebels. Such a rich reward might well have caused Forrest to turn his back on the army life he hated and with the willing and joyful help of his five allies, attempt to steal the shipment.

The Captain had set little store by the sergeant's remark, at the start of the escort duty, that such a crime was out of his league. For Forrest was not the kind of man it was easy to trust. Now, as Hedges swung from the saddle and sank to his boot-tops in the mud of the street, he eyed Forrest quizzically. "One day, you'll have to tell me why, sergeant," he muttered.

Forrest remained in the saddle and gave a shudder as the wind rose, gusting between the looming facades of the buildings. "If we live long enough," he said wryly, and spat into the mud. "Rebs don't get us, the pneumonia will."

Hedges cracked a cold smile. "You drop hints like they were thunderclaps, Forrest," he said, and trudged through the mud and up the steps of the courthouse, throwing up a salute in response to the present arms of the sentries.

"Hey, Frank!" Roger Bell yelled from back down the street. "My horse just crapped!"

"Only natural, Rog," John Scott shouted before Forrest could reply.

"It's what worries me," Bell retorted sourly. "We stand out here much longer in horse-droppings and mud with this rain, he's goin' to start sprouting roses from his ears and ass-hole!"

The laughter was short-lived. The men were tired, hungry and cold to their bones. The rain in their faces and turning the trails into quagmires had slowed progress to a crawl for most of the trip. They needed hot food, dry clothes and a leakproof roof over their heads. Humour didn't relieve their discomfort.

"Hotel across the street, sergeant!" Hedges called from the porchway of the courthouse. "There's food and beds for the drivers as well. Assign six men to guard the wagons. They'll be relieved in thirty minutes."

The sound of rain and wind made the rifle-shot seem far off. The scream of the sentry on Hedges' right wss much louder. He staggered back against the doorframe and looked down at the red hole over his right breast. Then his head snapped up and his scream became a cough. A great spray of bright crimson blood erupted from his gaping mouth and splashed across the courthouse steps.

"Suddenly, I ain't hungry!" Forrest yelled, springing down into the mud and jerking the Henry rifle from its boot as he came clear of the saddle.

Hedges snatched the rifle from the limp hands of the collapsing sentry and leapt forward, going into a dive which splashed him into the mud under the lead wagon.

"Jesus, he's dead!" the second sentry gasped as he stooped over the crumpled form.

"It could happen to you, you stupid – !" Forrest yelled as he wriggled under the wagon to join Hedges and the terrified driver.

A fusillade of rifle shots cut across the words. Two bullets exploded chunks of blood-dripping flesh from the face of the shocked man in the porch and he was flung through the doorway, dying without a sound.

"No one's got time to listen these days," Forrest growled.

Other men had died in the teeming rain which had suddenly been pierced by a lethal cross-fire of rifle bullets sent into the street by a twenty-strong unit of Rebel infantrymen positioned on the rooftops. A driver was caught in mid-air as he leapt from his wagon. The bullet merely glanced off his skull, erupting a lot of blood but not causing a fatal wound. He suffocated while unconscious, lying face down in the street and breathing thick mud into his windpipe. Two Negroes were blasted from their saddles, one dying instantly with a bullet in his brain as the other clutched at his stomach and died watching the blood ooze up between his tightly-clasped fingers.

By the time the second crackle of massed gunfire exploded from the rooftops, the Union soldiers and three surviving drivers were behind cover of some form or another. Scott, Bell and three ex-slaves crouched under the second wagon in the line, listening to the struggling, liquid breathing of the dying driver. Manfred had used his enormous bulk to crash down the doorway of a store. Rhett had charged in after him, followed by a half-dozen Negroes. Another freed slave, hit in the hand and more terrified than pained, had dived headfirst through the window of a pharmacy on the other side of the street. A shard of glass had ripped open his throat. He had collapsed on the floor, not quite dead. Seward went through the window after him, feet first. His heel had smashed down on to the pulped, blood-pulsing flesh, squeezing the final breath of life from the man.

"Watch where you're stepping!" Douglas yelled as he followed Seward through the window.

"How am I supposed to see a nigger in the frigging dark?" the youngster snarled, swinging around to crouch by the window, rifle aimed through it.

The ex-slaves – raw recruits and lacking battle experience – began firing wildly. The white troopers bided their time. More rifle fire exploded against the hiss of rain. Pale, ephemeral splashes of light showed along the uneven rooflines at each side of the street. Even as mud spurted, wood splinters flew and window glass shattered from the Rebel gunfire, the white troopers aimed and their Henry repeaters spat lead towards invisible targets. Two men screamed. One pitched forward from the roof and folded his body over the hitching rail outside the hotel across from the courthouse. Blood dripped from his forehead wound and turned the water in a puddle from black to red. Then he slid off the rail and crumpled headfirst into the coloured pool.

"He sure went out with a splash," Forrest muttered, levering a fresh shell into the breech.

"You still not hungry, sergeant?" Hedges asked as a renewed burst of gunfire sounded, opened from the roofs and answered from the street.

A Negro standing beside Manfred in the store doorway slumped to the ground. Manfred growled and fired his Henry at the maximum rate, sending three bullets through the rain. Two

27

grey-uniformed men fell from the roof of the pharmacy. One of them, wearing sergeant's chevrons, tried to crawl into cover. Seward and Douglas fired in unison. The Rebel's head exploded blood, flesh and bone chippings.

"Two whites for one black, that's almost a bargain," Manfred told the cowering Rhett with a grin.

Apart from being a fag, the New Englander was also a coward. "Billy and Hal had to finish off what you started!" he flung at the grinning Negro.

"Hush your mouth, man," the massive Manfred warned, still grinning as a hail of bullets tore wood splinters from the doorframe. "You're found dead, who'll know whether you was hit by a Johnnie Reb or one of us boys?"

Two men at the window looked at Rhett with eagerness in their eyes. The tall white man gulped and pressed himself hard against a heap of burst sacks which had spilled putrid grain.

"You wouldn't?" he gasped.

Manfred sighed. "I guess not."

Rhett sniggered his relief.

"But I'm a lousy guesser," Manfred added quickly, then whirled to blast another burst through the doorway.

"Well, what about it?" Hedges asked.

The officer and the non-com looked at each other. Their teeth and the whites of their eyes seemed brighter against the covering of mud clinging to their grizzled faces. The petrified wagon driver swung his gaze back and forth between the two men. All three flattened themselves into the mud as gunfire crackled and bullets ploughed into the ground, the wagon and one of the horses hitched to the wagon. The animal collapsed with a snort. Its partner struggled to get free, splashing great spumes of mud and water.

"You know a quiet little place around here, Captain?" Forrest asked wryly.

Hedges raised his head and spat his mouth clean. "It ain't ever goin' to be quiet until they've wiped us out," he replied. "Unless we do something better than lie here shooting at gun flashes."

A bullet whined down from a roof, glanced off a wheel rim

and burrowed into the heart of the driver. His expression changed from terror to surprise. Then he hid his face in the mud. Hedges' cold eyes viewed the death with utter detachment.

"It's bad to die on an empty stomach," the Captain said.

"You got something in mind?" Forrest asked.

"Yeah," Hedges replied. "A beef steak in a gallon of gravy."

"You set the juices running, Captain," Forrest muttered. "But my appetite'd be even better if I knew what you knew. Like, if I was sure old Robert E. Lee ain't got half the frigging Rebel army perched up on those roofs?"

"What the hell for?" Hedges snarled, and suddenly his eyes went from cold to hot, brighter than ever against the black mud with the light of anger.

A laugh ripped from Forrest's cruel mouth. It was loud enough to sound above the roar of guns. "So the guys in the courthouse told you we been had?" he rasped.

Hedges looked away from the contemptuous grin on the blackened face, and held his breath, tensing his body as he waited for the gunfire to subside. When it did, he launched himself forward, snaking out from under the wagon and throwing himself up into a crouch. Mud sucked at his boots, seeking to root him to the spot. But rage and the determination to survive powered the strength that took him in a fast, weaving run up on to the sidewalk and crashing into the hotel doors. They were flung open under his driving weight. He hurled himself to the side, hitting the floor and rolling. Bullets had reached for him every inch of the way. They whined in through the open doors and peppered the floorboards.

Sure the guys in the courthouse had told him. A shavetail lieutenant with spots and a simpering smile, and a paunchy Pinkerton agent who talked about the food and beds at the hotel as if they represented heaven on earth. They'd told him that the wagon train he and his men had taken from under the blazing guns of Quantrill's Raiders, then dragged hundreds of miles through knee-deep mud was a decoy. The gold had been shipped along another route while Hedges and his troopers escorted wagons pressed down into the moist, sucking earth by crates of lead bars.

It had been an excellent plan – made perfect because it had worked. The gold ingots had reached Washington in safety. The shavetail was pleased about the military success. The Pinkerton man was pleased that his agency had been involved in the tactic. As a soldier and an officer, Hedges had appreciated the soundness of the plan. The enemy had been fooled and that was all a part of war. That he and the men he commanded had borne the brunt of misdirected enemy attacks was also in the pattern of war. Even that he had not been told the real reason for his mission did not rankle him. Officers of higher rank than Captain were often required to carry out orders without being given reasons.

There was another pause in the firing. Then a renewed burst. Feet crashed on the sidewalk and Forrest dived through the doorway, hit the floor and rolled. He finished up on the opposite side of the narrow lobby from Hedges. More chips of wood spat up from the floorboards. A lamp flickered on a low wick above the reception desk. Its light reflected on the sergeant's discoloured teeth.

"They told me," Hedges grunted, getting to his feet and flattening himself against the wall, his slitted eyes moving from the rain-curtained doorway, to the desk, to the stairway angling up the rear wall and the restaurant entrance on Forrest's side of the lobby. "You already knew, right? You took a look in one of the crates. That's why you played the good soldier."

Forrest was making his own examination of the lobby, the Henry's barrel swinging ahead of his eyes, finger curled around the trigger. He spoke above the crackle of gunfire out on the street. "More than one, Captain," he replied. "What would I do with all that lead?"

This was what rankled with Hedges. That his sergeant had known about the freight for most of the trip: had undoubtedly derived a great deal of enjoyment in the knowledge that his commanding officer was in the dark and experiencing a heavy weight of anxiety that was completely groundless.

"You and the boys have fun?" the Captain asked, moving along the wall towards the desk.

Forrest peered into the restaurant and saw that a number of

tables had been pushed together and were spread with food – cold cuts, tureens of soup still giving off whisps of steam, plates of crackers and pots of coffee. "Just me," he answered, and swung around to lock his gaze with that of the officer.

"Am I supposed to be grateful?" Hedges snarled.

Forrest matched the tone. "Just learn, kid," he countered from his age seniority of ten years – thirty-eight to twenty-eight. "When you take a job, cover all the angles."

The hardness remained in Forrest's eyes, but his lips curled into a grin that was not altogether cynical. It was almost like an invitation to share mutual respect between equals: the older man showing he was prepared to make allowances for the inexperience of the younger one. This was not the first time the sergeant had attempted to bridge the rank gap and establish an affinity with Hedges – a man who on other occasions he had come close to killing.

"I'll remember," Hedges allowed against the background of rifle and revolver shots stabbing through the hiss of rain. But neither his tone nor his expression offered encouragement to the man across the lobby.

Forrest shrugged. "What they tell you about this crumby town?"

Hedges spat towards the spittoon, and missed. "We're on our own. There's a couple of civilians around somewhere."

"I'm one of 'em," a voice spoke up nervously.

Hedges and Forrest whirled towards the desk, levelling their rifles.

"Come up slow!" the Captain ordered. "Hands first."

The hands showed above the desk, trembling badly. The face that appeared between the arms was thin and white, with wide, red-veined eyes and a slack mouth that trickled the saliva of fear. He was about twenty and stopped growing from behind the desk when he reached a height of an inch or so above five feet. "Don't shoot, fellers!" he pleaded. "I'm on your side. I fixed the food for you men."

"That's what they told me," Hedges said. "Most of the civilians headed south when the Rebels were chased out. Army took over the town. Yesterday there were better than five hundred infantry and artillery here. They were moved west. A lieutenant, the two sentries that got blasted and a Pinkerton man were left to fill us in."

"Big of 'em!" Forrest rasped. "Were they filled in about the bastards up on the roofs?"

"They knew there was a chance that some Rebs were in the area," the Captain answered. "They didn't think they were very close."

The window to the right of the doorway was shattered and the trembling clerk threw himself down behind the desk as bullets smacked into the key board behind him.

"They're close!" Forrest growled.

"Close enough," Hedges countered. "Hey, you!"

"I ain't standing up no more!" the clerk yelled.

A further burst of firing, accompanied by a high scream of agony, sent a spattering of bullets through the doorway and window. Plaster spat from the wall close to Forrest, who went down into a crouch.

"He ain't very big, but he's smart," the sergeant muttered, then raised his voice as he looked across at the officer. "I'm getting dry in here, Captain. But that's all I'm getting. You figured out what we're goin' to do yet?"

"I'm thinking about it," Hedges replied, and he was. The crazy dash from the wagon into the hotel had been an impulsive act, born out of anger and nurtured by a selfish need to get away from the smirking object of his ire. But now he had shaken free of purely personal emotion. He was an officer responsible for the safety of his men. Forrest had put into words what all the troopers must be thinking.

"You can talk sitting down!" Hedges called to the cowering clerk. "Tell me about this town."

"Christ!" Forrest muttered, staying in a crouch as he moved into the restaurant. He scuttled across to the spread of food and went under the tables, taking a large cut of beef with him. He sat, cross-legged, chewing the meat from the bone as he listened to the voices of the clerk and the Captain.

Outside in the rain, the battle continued. Every horse in the wagon teams was dead. The cavalry mounts were either inert heaps in the mud or had bolted. The Negroes had been reduced in number to ten. The eight casualties were either crumpled on the street or sprawled in pools of their own blood at doorways and windows. Four Confederate soldiers had toppled from the rooftops. Three others lay still behind their inadequate cover with the rain diluting their spilled blood. But because of the wind-slanted rain and the thicker darkness of night which had rolled over the town in the wake of evening, no soldier on either side had a full view of what had happened. Most saw only blurred outlines of buildings and wagons and fired at gun flashes.

"Where the hell's Hedges?" Scott growled, flattening himself into the mud as bullets smacked into the wagon above him.

"You wanna go find out?" Bell asked him.

"Let's send one of them."

His thumb jerked towards the three ex-slaves sharing the cover of the wagon. The Negroes looked at each other and reached agreement without exchanging a word. They even elected a spokesman with their eyes.

"You wanna try, white trash?" the designated man hissed.

Three mud-covered rifles were suddenly trained on Scott and Bell. Scott swallowed hard.

"Guess not," Bell said.

Seward and Douglas were no longer inside the pharmacy. They had gone up the stairs, found an exit on to the roof and picked off one Rebel across the street. But neither was prepared to make the leap that would take them onto the roof of the bank next door to look for new targets. For such a move would have exposed them.

"Whatever's on those wagons ain't mine!" Seward justified.

"Captain smart-ass Hedges is in charge of it," Douglas pointed out. "You reckon he's got something in mind?"

Seward grimaced. "If he has, he sure don't seem anxious to let it out."

In the store, Rhett kept a tight grip on his unfired rifle and silently implored Hedges, God and the Union army to put an end to his terror. One of the Negroes at the window was dead and the other was bleeding badly from a chest wound. His ragged breathing was an ominous sound filling the brief pauses

33

between the shooting. At the door, Manfred alternately fired at the unseen enemy and scowled at the petrified Rhett.

"Hey, you Johnnie Rebs up there!"

Hedges' voice, the words shouted as loud as he was able, blasted through the rain in the wake of an angry burst of gunshots. The beating of the rain was all the answer he received for several long moments. In this period, the startled Forrest tossed away the remains of the meat and scuttled out into the lobby, suddenly aware that it was some time since Hedges and the desk clerk had said anything. The clerk's eyes were very frightened as they peered out over the top of the desk.

"Where'd he go?" the sergeant snapped.

A trembling hand appeared to point towards a door under the stairway. "Back way."

"Where to?"

Gulp. "Dunno, sergeant. But he seemed pretty interested in the flour mill half a block down the street."

Forrest's eyes showed how puzzled he was as he spun around and moved towards the front door of the hotel, careful to stay out of direct line of fire. He crouched down, with his rifle at the ready.

"You hear me?" Hedges yelled.

Not a shot had been fired since he shouted the first time. Again, the hissing of the rain was the only blemish on the silence as he listened for a response. It had been easy to get into the mill, for all the ambushers were concentrating their attention on the street. He had left the hotel through the kitchen door and moved silently across the back lots, occasionally hearing the scrape of boot leather on wood or a whisper of conversation above him. But without knowing the numerical strength of the enemy he was not prepared to try picking them off one by one.

"I hear you. You wanna give up?"

The flour mill was on a corner lot, almost half a block up from the hotel and courthouse which marked the northern extreme of the attackers' positions. The big side doors through which the grain was taken in and the sacks of flour sent out, were closed but not locked. Once inside, he struck a succession of matches to discover the layout of the building.

34

"You got it right!" he shouted.

The mill, perhaps the whole town, had been deserted in a hurry. There were a couple of wagonloads of grain piled by two hoppers at the rear. At the front was a huge pile of sacks. When his razor slit one open, freshly milled flour spilled out.

"Speak for your goddamn self, Hedges!" Roger Bell shouted. "I got my fill of stinking Reb prison."

"Damn right!" Billy Seward yelled.

"What'd you say, Frank?" John Scott demanded.

Forrest didn't hesitate. "You bastards better listen to the Captain!" he bellowed.

"You Yankees done yakking yet?" the officer in command of the attackers wanted to know.

Hedges was standing inside and to the right of the open front door of the mill. "We've done!" he shouted, trying to pin-point the position of the man who was replying to him. He thought he was on the roof of the express office next door to the courthouse. "My men will lay down their weapons and fall in outside the hotel." There was a babble of discontent, audible through the sound of the rain. Hedges ignored it. "Who am I talking to?"

"Major Collins, Second Kentucky Infantry," came the reply.

"Do I have your word my men will be accorded their due rights as prisoners of war, Major?"

There was no hesitation. "You have it."

"Sergeant!" Hedges roared.

"Sir?" Forrest answered.

"Fall in the men. Disarmed. Hands on their heads."

"Sir!" came the shouted response. Only the frightened desk clerk heard the rasping: "I sure hope you know what you're doing."

Forrest rested the Henry against the wall, then drew his Colt and dropped it on the floor. He took a deep breath and stepped outside, hooding his eyes against the rain and tensing his muscles in preparation to meet the thud of a bullet. No shot was fired. He moved off the sidewalk and peered down the street. "You heard the Captain!" he bellowed. "Get up off your butts and into line."

For stretched seconds, nothing happened. Then there was

the squelching sound of men raising themselves from the moist grip of mud. First Scott and Bell moved into the faint wedge of light slabbed into the street from the gaping entrance of the hotel. The Negroes who had been under the wagon with them were next to show. All had left their rifles behind and their holsters were empty.

"Hands on your heads!" Forrest rasped.

They complied, their faces showing the disgust they felt at the humiliation of the surrender. Four more Negroes trudged through the mud and joined the line. Then Manfred and Rhett. Seward and Douglas were trailed by two more Negroes and a second rank was formed.

"What the – " Seward started.

"Save it!" Forrest rasped.

"It done, sergeant?" Hedges called, his voice sounding more distant than before.

"I got a count of sixteen, sir," the non-com reported. "Makes it we lost eight."

Hedges was covered from the top of his forage cap to the toes of his boots in a thick layer of flour, the particles glued to him by the understrata of mud. The interior of the mill was filled with a heavy mist of flour, generated as he used his razor to slash the sacks, which he then hurled in every direction. As the sacks sailed through the air, they trailed arcs of the choking white dust. And as they hit walls and floor, they burst and great clouds of flour billowed up. Because of the fine powder clogging his nostrils and threatening to attack his throat if he opened his mouth, the Captain was unable to acknowledge Forrest's shout until he was out on the street, with the door firmly closed behind him. He carried an unlit lamp plucked from a low beam.

"March the men this way, sergeant!" he ordered, then dashed across the street and into the shelter of a livery stable on the opposite corner.

Forrest had learned never to be surprised at what Hedges did or the orders he gave. "Turn left, quick march!" he snapped, using the tone of voice which the troopers had learned to obey instantly.

The two unequal lines of bedraggled uniformed figures had

made the turn and were marching awkwardly through the mud before the men on the roof had recovered from their surprise.

"What the hell!" Major Collins exploded. "Hey, you men!"

Because of the rain-streaked murk, only those Rebels positioned on the roofs of the hotel and the courthouse could see what was happening. The others could hear, but no order had been given.

"Halt!" the Major yelled. "Halt or we fire!"

Forrest peered ahead and strained his ears for an order from Hedges. He saw and heard nothing. The men continued the trudging march, each one of them holding his breath.

"Captain?" the sergeant shouted.

"Halt I say!" the Rebel officer ordered, standing up. The four men on the courthouse with him raised themselves, rifles levelled. Three more figures loomed up from behind the hotel sign.

Another two squelching paces. Sweat mingled with the rain on the strained faces, helping to wash the flesh clear of mud.

"Captain, what do we do?"

The head of the column was within ten yards of the corner. Hedges cursed under his breath at the slowness with which the men were ploughing through the ankle-deep mud. But he knew he could wait no longer.

"Run!" he yelled, with a glance across the street.

He saw the mill's window was still acting as a barrier to the thick, white mist. Then the men were running, stumbling and crashing into each other in their panic to get from under the guns of momentarily surprised Rebel soldiers. Hedges got off three rapid shots towards the hotel roof and heard a scream before the Rebels opened fire. Bullets splatted into mud and thudded into flesh. Three of the Negroes went down. Two lay still. The third sat up and tried to lift himself. But blood gushed from his thigh. He grasped his legs in both hands. The others — black and white — splashed around him. His head exploded into ghastly fragments as a hail of bullets was pumped into it. Another Negro went down and was still.

The survivors ploughed between the mill and livery, staring in horror at the white apparition that was Hedges.

"Keep running!" the Captain ordered, hurling his rifle.

Forrest caught the weapon and set the pace.

"After them!" Major Collins roared. "Don't let them get away!"

The Union troopers struggled across the street junction, harried by a group of four shots. Only one found a mark and Manfred sat down hard, gushing blood from a shattered ankle. He was immediately outside the door of the mill. In the short period of silence while the Rebels jumped and clambered down from their rooftop positions to give chase, the massive Negro stared at Hedges with an odd mixture of anguish and puzzlement in his wide eyes. He saw the Captain pick up the lamp and back into the depths of the livery. Hedges gave a quick shake of his head. Manfred got the message and stared down at his wound.

The Rebel soldiers had as much difficulty to make speed through the mud as the Union men. When Hedges saw the first one pass, he struck a match and lit the lamp wick. A small group of five or six, with the Major among them, slogged into sight. Hedges replaced the lamp glass. Two shots were fired – wildly because the targets were lost in the rain and dark. A Rebel soldier caught the flash of light from the corner of his eye and swung his head around to stare into the livery. Manfred stuck out his good leg and the soldier went headlong into the mud with a cry of alarm.

Hedges drew the Colt with his free hand and started to run forward. The flame of the lamp danced crazily in the glass. He halted abruptly in the doorway and hurled the lamp. It arced across the street, spinning wildly. The flame died, then flared again. A succession of images were channelled into Hedges' mind through the slits of his hooded eyes. The face of Manfred, showing terror, hatred, then foregiveness. A dozen, perhaps more, of grey-uniformed figures frozen momentarily into a variety of attitudes of awkward running. A rifle pointed towards him. The man with the rifle being flung backwards as the Colt exploded a bullet into his heart. The lamp smashing through the white backed window, flaring brighter than ever as if in triumph at defeating the attempt of the pelting rain to extinguish it. Then there was just darkness as he flung himself to the ground behind the protective front wall of the stable.

The sound of the explosion was like a thousand cannon fired simultaneously. The orange flames lit up the entire town for a brief moment. The blast disintegrated the mill. Men were lifted bodily from the mud and tossed back again or smashed against the walls of surrounding buildings. There were no screams, for there was no time. Flesh was burst open like the skin of rotten fruit. Entrails and dismembered limbs – even severed heads – sailed through the night air, fleetingly devoid of rain under the force of the searing blast.

The sound seemed to roll on and on in Hedges' mind. It affected his sense of balance and it was only at the third attempt that he was able to haul himself erect and peer out on to the street. The ruined mill blazed with an angry crackling noise, sending up tongues of flame to do battle with the teeming rain. Its light sprayed out against the night, putting the ghastly tableau of bleeding and burned flesh on cruel display.

Hedges viewed it without emotion, his slitted eyes raking the scene for a sign of life, the Colt swinging to left and right: ready to put out the slightest spark if it showed. But only the flames and the rain provided movement on the street. All else was still. Manfred had been cut in half by a piece of flying debris. His head was twisted in the attitude of a broken neck and his eyes were directed towards the Captain. They were as cold and devoid of feeling as were Hedges.

Suddenly, the officer whirled to the left as the roaring subsided in his head and he heard another sound. His knuckle was white as his finger pressured the trigger of the Colt. But he was as skilled in the art of not killing as he was in the taking of life. The shavetail lieutenant and the Pinkerton man were moving down the street, keeping to the sidewalk. On the other side, the terrified desk clerk was peering towards the scene of slaughter. When the familiar noise of mud sucking at boots sounded from the other direction, Hedges turned more slowly. Twelve troopers trudged into the area lit by the flames, equally divided, black and white. Five of the whites surveyed the broken and mutilated bodies with expressions ranging from simple delight to giggling

39

glee. Rhett clasped his hands in front of him to stop them trembling. The rest of his body shook uncontrollably. The Negroes looked for and found the recognizable portion of Manfred. They halted and stared at their dead leader in silent sadness.

"You did all right, Captain," Forrest complimented.

"Obliged," Hedges replied sardonically. He slid the Colt back into its holster and held out his hands.

Forrest tossed the Henry to him and he caught it. "Pretty risky, though." He waved his hand to encompass the scene of carnage. "Could have been us as well as them."

Hedges shrugged and started back towards the hotel. "Sometimes you can't cover all the angles."

The Pinkerton man, the lieutenant and the hotel clerk looked at the troopers with amazement showing through their horror, unable to understand the casual acceptance of such bloody and wholesale death.

"I reckon," Forrest agreed, falling in beside the Captain. "Just the one that put you in a nice safe place when the crap hit the fan."

"You griping?" Hedges snapped.

Forrest grinned. "Do I ever? Let's eat."

The other whites moves off towards the hotel.

"Captain!" the Pinkerton man called. "You considered what we said earlier?"

"I been busy," Hedges answered flatly. "I think better on a full stomach."

"You're all invited, too," the lieutenant told the ex-slaves, who stood with heads bowed among the mutilated corpses.

"First we bury our dead," a man replied, his voice heavy with grief.

Seward sniggered and shot a glance towards Rhett. "Maybe we ought to send Bob to the funeral," he muttered. "Ain't much, but a pansy's all we got."

Raucous laughter greeted the comment as the New Englander scowled and the Negroes showed hate in their eyes. Hedges was about to bawl out the men but then he felt his attention drawn towards the top half of Manfred's body. In the flickering light of the fire, the black man's eyes were no longer cold. The reflected flames seemed to be feeding on the fuel of the dead man's enraged hate. Not for the first time in the war, Hedges was conscious of the fact a mixture of self-pity and sympathy for others offered an easy outlet for his emotions. But at the same time he knew this was a luxury he could not afford – for the easy way was the way of weakness. And at the first sign of weakness, his tenuous authority over the men would be wiped out. He elected to drive back his true feelings with a wedge of cynicism.

"He looks more like a shrinking violet," he muttered, his harsh eyes causing the wretched Rhett to flinch. "We got nothing we can send." He nodded towards the burning mill, with the flames lessening in intensity under the assault of the rain. "That's where all the flour's gone."

EDGE had a second floor front room in the St. David's Hotel. It was as neat and clean as everything else about the town of Jerusalem, furnished with a single bed, a clothes closet and a bureau. There was a Bible on the bureau, bearing an inscription which marked it as a donation from the ubiquitous Sam Lynch.

Edge took his much-needed rest lying on top of the bed covers, fully-dressed except for his hat, boots and gunbelt. The Colt was clutched in his right hand. The Winchester was on the floor, the lever action and trigger less than an inch from where his left hand trailed over the side of the bed. He slept in the manner of a man accustomed to expect danger at any moment, his posture suggesting that he would be able to snap upright and level both guns in a split-second should a threat present itself. There even seemed to be a sliver of blue and white visible beneath each shuttered eyelid.

But on this shallow level of sleep, his highly-developed sixth sense was able to differentiate between the innocent sounds and those which might signal danger. Thus, while he would undoubtedly have whipped to full awareness had the door handle squeaked or the window been eased open, the din of preparation for Sam Lynch's birthday celebration failed to rouse him from his refreshing, dream-free sleep.

When he did awake, it was automatically, after his body and mind had taken sufficient rest. It just so happened that the church bells were tolling at the same time, ringing out over the sunlit town and the verdant country all around, warning the citizens that the midday service was imminent. He pulled on his boots and buckled his gunbelt into place before moving to the window. His eyes, narrowed against the bright sunlight, expressed no surprise at what they saw.

The single street of Jerusalem was decked out with streamers and flags, balloons and colourful mobiles. The bunting was draped across the fronts of buildings and strung from ropes spanning the street. And from every building and each rope there hung a portrait of a dour-faced man in a stovepipe hat and high winged collar. Edge guessed the pictures were of Sam Lynch.

Beneath the decorations, which fluttered fitfully in a slight breeze, the citizens moved towards the church. The men wore their Sunday-best suits, the women tried to outdo each other in flouncy finery and the children looked as if they would rather be in patched levis than the go-to-meeting clothes.

On the way to church, the faithful passed under the start-finish sign of the Sam Lynch Horse Race, moved across the front of the Sam Lynch Bandstand, went around one side on a staked out ring for the Sam Lynch Prize Fight and weaved among various stalls and booths housing games and amusements for young and old.

Edge watched the scene for a few moments, spotting Sheriff Pitman with his arm in a sling, escorting his sour-faced wife, Harvey the bartender, the two customers who had been in the saloon, and the barber. Then he put on his hat, picked up the Winchester and left the room. As he moved along the landing and started down the stairway, he sensed the emptiness of the hotel. The lobby was deserted to the extent that there was no clerk behind the desk. After banging the call bell without response, Edge peeled two dollars off his bankroll and laid them on the register. He wrote *Paid* beside his name.

Outside, the street was less crowded. Just the latecomers, hurrying towards the church as the final note of the bell rolled away across the cattle-dotted pasture into the distant hills. When the big, nail-studded door closed behind them, the sense of desolation clamped down over the whole town. Edge's footfalls had a hollow ring on the sidewalk as he headed for the restaurant door. Then an organ burst into melodious life and massed voices were raised in a hymn.

The restaurant was as empty as the hotel. A large banner was strung across one wall: EAT HEARTY ON SAM LYNCH. The free food was arrayed on a long trestle table. Edge selected stew with dumplings followed by apple pie and cream. The coffee was as good as the food. He ate the meal to the accompaniment of hymns interspersed with prayers and a sermon. The service showed no sign of finishing as he left the restaurant and moved slowly down the street towards the livery. He checked that his horse had been taken care of and that the saddle and bedroll had not been tampered with. Then he went further down the street and tried the door of the barber's shop. It was unlocked. Inside there was just the one chair positioned before a sink with a mirror above. He sat down and waited.

The church service ended with a prolonged period of personal meditation in absolute silence. Then life returned to Jerusalem. Adult laughter and the yells of children broke through the peace as the congregation flowed out on to the street. A couple of pistol shots cracked and the church bells began to ring with a more joyful note than before. Hoofbeats bounced between the building facades. Barkers shouted the attractions of the various sideshows.

Edge looked in the mirror and saw the surprised look on the old barber's face as the man entered.

"Hey, nobody works on Sam Lynch's birthday, mister," the man complained. But then he found himself trapped by the hooded-eyed stare reflected in the mirror. "But I guess whiskers still grow, uh?"

Edge rasped a hand over his thickly stubbled chin and the old man moved forward and started his preparations for a shave. He kept glancing down at the Winchester resting across the arms of the chair. Edge made no attempt to move the rifle when the barber draped a cover over him.

"Who's Sam Lynch?"

The barber poured boiling water into a mug and started to whip up a lather. He shot several glances towards the door, open to admit the sounds of celebration. "Town's founder, mister. A real rich Englishman. Seems the English got this kinda hymn about building Jerusalem in England's green and pleasant land. Trouble was, old Sam had to leave England. Seems he got rich by unfair means. Come to this country and the religion bug bit him."

The barber began to lather Edge's face, taking great care not to get soap in the narrowed eyes.

"Built this town and the farms out there on the range. Used near all his ill-gotten gains on doin' it. Kinda makin' restitution for his sins, I guess. When it was all built he give it away to whoever happened along. Trouble was, a couple of his country-men showed up gunning for him. Seems they was the business partners he run out on. Blasted him — both at the same time with double-barrelled shotguns. Weren't enough of old Sam left to make any last wishes. So Mr. Rawlings the banker, Sheriff Pitman and the pastor from the church, they got together and figured out the idea of the birthday celebration every year. Rest of the time, folks act real peaceful and attend to their chores. But on old Sam's birthday, they let their hair down."

The barber shaved Edge as he told the story.

"What happened to the two fellers who killed him?" Edge asked as the residue of lather was gently mopped from his face.

The old man's watery eyes filled with sadness. "Folks don't talk about that. They didn't die easy, mister. If you happen to ride through a certain clearing in the pine forest south of here, you'll probably find their bones still hanging from the tree they was hung from — upside down." He carefully took the covering from his customer. "It's like for three-hundred-and-sixty-four days of the year, the folks have to work to forget what they did to those fellers. Only on old Sam's birthday do they cut loose."

Edge leaned towards the mirror and ran a hand over his freshly-shaven features. Although the removal of the stubble should have made him look younger, it didn't. For now the deep lines of hardship showed up clearly in the copper-coloured flesh and there was not a trace of youth to be seen. "How much?" he asked, getting to his feet.

The old man shook his head. "I get a free meal today, so I can afford to give a free shave."

"Obliged," Edge said, and headed for the door.

The old man scuttled out after him without waiting to clear up, and hurried down the street, turning into the saloon. Edge sat in the rocking chair on the stoop before the shop and rolled a cigarette. There were a lot more people milling among the amusements than could possibly live in the town or on the farmsteads surrounding it. He guessed the poster at the old line cabin and possibly others spread around the country had attracted the strangers. There were a great many of these, notable for their workaday clothes and unscrubbed faces and hands.

For an hour, Edge rested easy in the rocker, watching the start and finish of the horse race, then listening with disinterest to the ten-man band falter through a limited repertoire. The prize fight was being staged at the far end of the street and initially it attracted little attention. But, as the afternoon wore on, the crowd around the ring began to expand, drawing on the well-fed and well-oiled floaters who had taken their fill of the other entertainments.

By the time Edge decided to check out the cause of the cheering and shouting at the far end of town, he was the only person showing any apparent interest in the band. He sensed the eyes of the musicians following him as he rose from the chair and ambled down the centre of the empty street. The middle-aged conductor half turned to send a pleading glance towards the tall half-breed.

"Keep practising, fellers," he called. "It's just gotta get better."

The conductor gave him a withering look and continued to brandish his baton. As Edge drew closer to the noisy crowd, the discordant music was swamped. He stepped up on to the sidewalk in front of the bank and his height enabled him to see across the heads of the excited audience. Both fighters were stripped to the waist and were dressed only in pants. One was the well-built youngster who had been in the saloon yesterday.

The other was an inch taller but was leaner. By the number of bruises on his sun-tanned body and the blood-spilling cuts on his face, his reach advantage was outweighed by the other man's speed. Despite the squashed nose, purple eye and ugly contusion on the taller man's face, Edge found something familiar about him.

"Like to make a bet, mister?"

Edge swung around and saw a familiar face he could place. It belonged to the painfully thin man who had been with the smaller fighter in the saloon. He carried a small notebook in one hand and a heavy looking leather bag in the other.

"Maybe," Edge said, and returned his attention to the fight as a raucous cheer was raised by the crowd.

The fighter getting the worst of the contest had just been pitched full length to the ground by a powerful jab into his stomach. The crowd was chanting for the beefy man to move in and end it.

"The boy on the deck is McNally," the thin man explained. "Right now I'm offering ten-to-one on him. The other fighter is Jefferson. Should be evens, but two-to-one to make it interesting."

Edge seemed to ignore the speaker, as he watched McNally haul himself to his feet before the dancing Jefferson. Jefferson weaved in and telegraphed a left hook. McNally countered it instinctively, much to the disappointment of the crowd. He threw a weak right that had no chance of connecting. Jefferson swung a roundhouse that crunched into McNally's cheek. McNally went down to a roar of approval. It seemed to use a lot of energy to get him to his feet again – too much, like the first time.

"Two grand on McNally," Edge said softly, swinging to face the man making book and curling back his lips in a grin as he saw the surprise inscribed on the lean features.

"That much on an outsider?" The man blinked and swallowed hard.

Edge extracted his bankroll and peeled off the required number of bills. The roll had been a great deal fatter a few months ago. But buying a spread and getting married had cost money.

"Write the slip before my boy comes in from the outside," Edge ordered softly.

The thin man did so, with a shaking hand and gave the slip to Edge. He stuffed the money into the bag already fat with bills, and made to move away.

"Hold it, feller," Edge warned. The Colt was in his holster and the rifle was sloped casually across his shoulder. But the cold blue eyes glinted through their slits in a threat as potent as any gun muzzle. He moderated his tone. "Be obliged if you stayed where I can see you."

The thin man blinked and tried to sound irate. "Don't you trust me?"

"Man has to earn trust," Edge replied, turning his head to watch the fight. "But I ain't paying those kind of wages unless I'm sure you're a hard worker, feller."

There was a roar as McNally went down again, clutching at his groin. Edge watched impassively as the youngster writhed in apparent agony. But on the periphery of his vision he could see the shadow of the thin man. The thin man knew this, so he made no move. McNally started to rise slowly, his battered face formed into a mask of anguish. Jefferson ignored the screams and yells of the crowd. He was going through the motions of weaving and crouching, preparing for the kill, but his heart wasn't in it. His eyes swung from side to side, searching for somebody in the crowd. As he glanced towards the bank, Edge side-stepped in front of the thin man.

McNally leapt to his feet with a power and litheness which bore no relation to the marks of the beating he showed. He feinted to the left, blocked a roundhouse and sent a piledriving jab into Jefferson's exposed stomach. Jefferson began to fold forward. McNally started an uppercut from way down and connected with every ounce of his strength. Something clicked in Jefferson's jaw. The man was lifted inches from the ground, his body ramrod stiff for a second. Then, in front of the crowd struck dumb by the shock, he thudded his bare feet against the ground. His legs gave way and he crumpled. He became inert.

McNally forced open his split lips in a grin of triumph. The crowd found its collective voice and screamed at the senseless fighter to get up.

Edge swung around and trapped the trembling thin man with an ice-cold stare. "Two by ten makes twenty, feller," he said against the incensed roar of the crowd. "Plus my stake." The grin reached his mouth, but no higher. "Guess that puts the fixer in a fix, uh?"

A shotgun blasted the crowd into abrupt silence. All eyes except those of Edge swung to gaze up at the roof of the law office. A series of gasps hissed through the crowd. A shocked voice cut across the breathy sound: "It's Mrs. Pitman."

Now the tall half-breed looked up at the roof. The sheriff's wife had ceased to struggle against the grasp of a masked man who used his free hand to hold a revolver against her temple. A second masked man held a shotgun pointed skywards, with smoke still whisping from one of the two barrels. He lowered it to cover the upturned faces of the people on the street.

"We figure we got us a winning bet," the redhead with the shotgun called into the silence.

The man holding Mrs. Pitman cocked his revolver and the dry click sounded louder than the shouted words. The sheriff tore his gaze away from his wife's plight and swung around to survey the many faces now turned to stare at him. His features were twisted by anguish, the skin as white as the fabric of the sling around his arm. His eyes searched for and found the thin man, standing nervously beside Edge on the bank's stoop.

"Toss the money up to them!" the lawman croaked.

The thin man shot a frightened glance at Edge. "Do I give 'em the money?" he asked, his voice trembling as much as his hands.

The half-breed shrugged. "You make a lousy book," he muttered. "But they've got a good cover. Kinda puts you in a bind, don't it?"

CHAPTER FOUR

"Blast Jefferson Davis?" Forrest exclaimed. "In the middle of Richmond, for Christ sake!"

The white troopers were in the hotel restaurant, washing down their first hot meal in many days with coffee and brandy chasers. The survivors of the liberated slaves were still out in the slackening rain, attending to the burial of their dead. The Lieutenant, the Pinkerton man and the hotel clerk had watched with varying degrees of distaste as the travel and battle weary troopers had attacked the food. Not until the men had eaten their fill and achieved a state of easy relaxation had the detective shot a glance to Hedges and received a nod of approval.

The smooth-faced, round-bellied civilian was not a man to beat about the bush and his opening statement, as he sprang energetically to his feet, was as bald as his dome-like head: "We want you guys to go to the Confederate capital and put a few bullets into the Reb president."

Forrest was the only trooper to utter his reaction in words. Scott and Douglas gasped. Bell blinked, Seward sniggered and Rhett belched. Hedges smoked a cigarette as calmly as before. At the courthouse immediately after his arrival in Hartford Gap, the Lieutenant with the acned face had intimated the kind of assignment the army had in mind for Hedges and his men. But Hedges had interrupted the junior officer almost before he was started in order to ensure his men were fed and sheltered. The Rebel ambushers had extended the interruption.

"Naturally," the Pinkerton man went on. "For this kind of mission, we'd only consider using volunteers."

"Then you got the wrong outfit," Douglas growled.

Forrest glanced at Hedges, sitting across the table from him, and saw the attitude of easy listening the Captain had adopted. "Maybe he ain't, Hal," the sergeant said grimly.

"Hear the man out," Hedges muttered.

The Pinkerton detective nodded his appreciation of the attentive silence the Captain's remark brought about. "It wasn't by sticking a pin in a map that we chose this town as the end of the line for the decoy wagon train."

"Decoy!" Seward snorted.

Forrest swung around in his chair to grimace at the youngster. "Billy?" Pleasantly.

"Yeah, Frank?"

"You remember when the wagons kept getting bogged down in the mud and me and the Captain yelled at you guys to get the lead out?"

Seward was puzzled. "Sure, Frank."

Forrest's tone hardened. "We meant it. Now shut your goddamn mouth and listen."

Questions sprang to the lips of all five troopers who had learned the truth for the first time. But the mean eyes of the sergeant raking across their faces drove the queries back down their throats.

"Carry on, mister," Forrest invited.

"Thanks," the detective said, his impatience beginning to show. He began to speak more rapidly, as if anxious to get as much said as possible before the next interruption. "No, it was chosen by General Grant himself as the ideal jumping off point for a secret mission such as this. There were other Union held towns closer than this, but the Rebs are on the look-out for penetrations from them. From here, Richmond's better than three hundred miles away, most all of it's Rebel held. We figure they wouldn't expect trouble from this direction." He cleared his throat. "Leastways, until you got real close to the city."

"Easy on the *you* feller," Hedges said, grinding out the cigarette under his heel. "How many other outfits have you asked to volunteer?"

The Pinkerton man coloured and his collar seemed to shrink around his throat. His eyes transmitted a plea to the Lieutenant and the officer got to his feet.

"You and your men have had a great deal of experience in moving about behind enemy lines," the shavetail explained. "It was thought such experience would prove invaluable in—"

"No other outfit," Hedges growled.

The Lieutenant looked as if he was about to deny this, but then realized the futility of such a statement. "That's right, sir."

Forrest had been raking his teeth with a dirty fingernail. He found a piece of trapped meat and spat it out. "Nice to feel wanted," he muttered.

Something the detective had said was nagging at the back of Hedges' mind, but he couldn't put his finger on it. Everybody was waiting for him to make a more constructive comment than Forrest's. "Last time there was a difference," he said. "We didn't go sneaking through the Reb lines by choice. We got took." Then the telling phrase spoken by the Pinkerton man was flipped into the forefront of his mind. The lines of his lean face hardened and his eyes turned to ice. "And we got took again!" he hissed, his lips hardly moving.

The Lieutenant was suddenly as jittery as the detective. "Sir, I'd remind you that General Grant himself recommended you for this mission," he said hoarsely.

"You know something I don't!" Forrest said tersely, his mean eyes boring into the Captain's rigid profile.

"Only what I heard, sergeant," Hedges said softly, his cold eyed stare moving from the Lieutenant, to the detective, to the hotel clerk and back again. "I told you to listen. Awhile back, the eye that never sleeps said there *were* other Union held towns closer than this. *Were* is past tense."

"Christ!" Bob Rhett exclaimed.

The grammatical reference meant nothing to the others who were without the benefit of the kind of education enjoyed by Hedges and Rhett. But all knew the practical difference between was and were. The anger seemed to hover in the flickering lamp light above the troopers, then to move forward and press against the two civilians and the Lieutenant.

"We're only doing what we been told!" the shavetail blurted. "We're in the same kind of spot as you guys. The army took this town and were supposed to hold it until you got here. You were going to be given the choice of moving out with them, or heading for Richmond. But you were late getting here. The Rebs were coming. The army had to leave. What do you think it was like for us? Sitting here in the middle of country crawling with Johnnie Rebs?"

"Sympathy, he wants!" John Scott growled.

"Even worse for me," the hotel clerk put in, his voice high-pitched and quivering. "You wear a uniform, they get you and you're a prisoner of war. Me they'd shoot as a spy."

"Me, too," the detective added.

"My heart bleeds for you," Roger Bell grunted.

"Don't tempt providence, soldier," Hedges retorted as he got to his feet.

Forrest got up. "Wondered how long we were goin' on with this little dinner party," he muttered. "Considerin'."

"What you goin' to do?" the Pinkerton man asked anxiously.

"Check on some missing men," Hedges answered, picking up his rifle from where it rested against the table. "How long's it take to dig a few holes in ground as soft as this?"

"Hell, I forgot about the nig – the blacks," Douglas said softly, as he and the others hoisted their rifles.

"That's why you're only a corporal and not a Captain," Scott told him.

"Kinda wish Hal was the top hand," Rhett put in as he got unsteadily to his feet. "He'd tell those guys what to do with their mission."

Seward grinned. "Don't you think of anything else but – "

A bullet smashed through the window and shattered one of the two lamps hanging from a ceiling beam. Glass showered down over the hotel clerk. Blood sprang from a dozen small cuts on his face and he remained standing, screaming his shock as every other man in the room dived for the floor. A second shot sounded and more window glass tinkled. The hotel clerk stopped screaming and fell backwards. The signs of the many small cuts on his face were obliterated by the tide of blood which sprang from a hole in the centre of his forehead and cascaded over his dead flesh.

The silence was leaden. It made the men aware for the first time that the rain had ceased to fall. When they began to breathe again the rasping sound was amplified out of proportion for the first few moments.

"Rhett, the window!" Hedges whispered. "Scott and Douglas upstairs. Back and front. Bell, try to make the roof. Douglas and Forrest, first floor back."

The troopers moved off to take up their positions, first on their bellies and then raising on to all fours. As always, they were at their best under fire with specific orders to follow – except for Rhett. He reached the window and flattened himself against the floor, his hands clasped over his head as protection should more glass shower under the impact of a bullet.

"What about me and Mr. Marlowe?" the Lieutenant asked hoarsely.

Hedges prodded his rifle in the direction of the cowering New Englander. "Hold his hand," he rasped. "But be careful – it could be the start of something big."

He ignored the quizzical stares of the two men and snaked out into the lobby. The main doors were closed now and the light above the desk had been extinguished. He got to his feet and ran lightly to the front. The windows flanking the doors were of opaque glass. He crouched and slid the rifle to the far side. Then he sprang forward, gripped the handles, flung wide the doors and leapt out of the opening as three rifles cracked and bullets thudded against the frame. He snatched up the Henry and crouched. His narrow-angled view of the street showed him nothing but mud and rain-sodden building fronts.

"Hey, you, Captain feller!"

Hedges was momentarily surprised, for he recognized the voice. It belonged to the Negro who had announced the intention to bury his dead comrades.

"That's you in the doorway. I know it."

"We can smell you!" another voice called, and his accent was also deep and as dark brown as his skin. "You got the stink of a murderer on you, Captain feller."

Hedges continued to remain silent, his ears straining to pinpoint the positions of the men by the sounds of their voices. He

53

thought they were in the express office next to the courthouse. That part of the street was outside his range of vision.

"We held a meeting," the first black trooper called. "We don't like what happened to Manfred. He was good man. Helped us a lot when slaves. Helped you lot when free. You didn't oughta killed him, Captain feller. Okay in war if enemy kill. Lousy if own officer do it. You come out and we hang you. Others go free."

"You already blasted one of the others!" This from Rhett, his voice a terrified whine. It was muffled, as if he was still pressing his head hard against the floor.

"Unlucky shot!" came the reply. "Only mean to get attention. You come out here, Captain feller. Then we not attack. You not be blamed for killing more own men."

Hedges was no longer crouching by the open doorway. He had retreated back into the depths of the darkened lobby, crossed in front of the desk and then gone down onto his belly to snake into the lighted restaurant. Not until he began to drag the dead hotel clerk across the floor did he make any sound which drew the startled attention of the three men at the window. He interrupted his chore only long enough to crook a finger at them. They crawled among the tables and chairs and followed him out into the lobby.

Rhett was praying, his lips moving to form the words but not uttering them aloud. His eyes were screwed tight shut. The Lieutenant and Marlowe looked on in amazement as the Captain began to unfasten his tunic buttons.

"You comin' out, Captain feller? Or do we come in and get you?"

He punctuated the demand with a shot. Rhett groaned and pressed himself full length to the floor as the bullet thudded harmlessly into the wall. The Lieutenant concentrated hard on Hedges' thin lips. Like Rhett's a moment before, they moved to transmit silent words. But they were calling for help from a closer and far less divine source. The shavetail bobbed his head in acknowledgement and moved off in a crouch, going through the doorway leading to the rear of the hotel. When he reappeared, he was followed by Forrest and Douglas, who glanced quizzically at the men gathered around the inert form of the blood-run corpse. Then Hedges' cold eyes seemed to hasten their silent ascent of the stairway. The Lieutenant went with them.

"Answer me!"

The demand, harsh with impatience, cut into the silence just as the Pinkerton man gave a nod that he understood the Captain's mouthed instructions.

Upstairs, the Lieutenant and the troopers crowded into a front bedroom and flitted across to the window. Forrest moved to the front of the group and eased it up. Cold, damp air flowed into the room. The soldiers moved out, stepping silently on to the railed balcony and spreading along its length. Their eyes raked the street and saw the wagons with their dead teams still harnessed, the blank windows of the buildings and three, grey-clad, death rigid corpses. The flour mill was now a heap of blackened timber, every trace of the fire extinguished by the rain before it had stopped. The light level was low, supplied by the pale disc of a full moon just visible through thick cloud. Nothing moved beneath it. The troopers were too intent upon watching for a sign of the mutineers to concern themselves with the implications of what the Lieutenant had instructed: "The Captain says to come with me and do what comes naturally."

"I got him, sergeant!"

Already tense in expectancy of a hail of bullets whistling through the night, the troopers became rigid at the sudden, excited shout from Marlowe.

"I ain't goin' out to get hung!" This from Hedges, in a tone nobody had heard from him before – naked fear.

"Halt!"

"You wouldn't dare!"

Footfalls thudded against floorboards.

"Jesus, I'll kill you."

A rifle shot and a scream.

The troopers swung their eyes towards the Lieutenant. He shrugged.

"Hey, you out there!" Marlowe's voice was still pitched high with excitement.

"What's happened?" The newly appointed leader of the freed slaves sounded suspicious.

Every trooper on the balcony swung his attention to the open doorway of the express office from which the question had been shouted.

"It was him or us!" Marlowe called in reply. "Hedges is dead."

There was a pause. A murmur of conversation scratched it faintly. Then:

"Bring him out. All of you."

Another pause. Every rifle on the balcony was trained on the doorway of the express office. Six fingers were curled around triggers.

"Two of us," Marlowe yelled.

More whispered conversation.

"Okay. But any tricks, we shoot men who bring him. Men carry no weapons."

"It's a deal," came the reply without a hesitation. "We're comin'."

A rifle barrel was pushed out through the doorway across the street. It had an evil sheen in the pale light. Feet shuffled over the bare boards in the lobby. The sound was louder against the sidewalk.

"Centre of the street," the deep voice demanded.

Marlowe and Rhett splashed down into the mud, stepping around the puddle in which the dead Rebel soldier hid his face. The hotel clerk, attired in Hedges' uniform, was slung limply between them. Rhett was holding the dead legs and his trembling was transmitted to the lower half of the burden. He stumbled twice, to curses from Marlowe, and was covered from head to toe in fresh mud before the middle of the street was reached.

"What now, for Christ sake?" he shrieked after several tense seconds had slid silently by.

"Dumb bastards," Forrest rasped to himself as the six Negroes stepped from cover, three from the express office and three moving on to the steps of the courthouse beside the slumped bodies of the sentries. All their rifles were levelled at Marlowe and Rhett.

But it was the Henry of the Captain which exploded. Hedges was stretched out full-length on the floor of the lobby, aiming just over the trembling left shoulder of Rhett. The terrified New Englander felt the slip-stream of the bullet waft across his neck. He screamed and released his half of the burden as he flung himself into the mud. The bullet smashed through the broad nose of the mutineer's leader and the force of the impact sent him sprawling backwards through the doorway of the express office.

All except one of his men wasted a fatal split second in swinging their heads to see the effect of the surprise shot. The man on the far right fired. Marlowe looked down at the blood spouting from his chest. He released his grip on the body and tried to reach up at his wound. Death beat him and he crumpled. Unlike Rhett, he was unable to claw at the oozing mud to try to dig a hole for himself. A fusillade of shots sounded from the balcony. Black faces spurted blood and blue uniforms were suddenly stained by red blotches. Even as the Negroes screamed and started to fall, the white men pumped the lever actions of their repeaters and sent another hail of lead across the street. Pieces of flesh and splinters of bone spun away amid sprays of blood. For a moment, as metal scraped against metal, the slumped forms were inert. A third burst of concentrated fire caused dead flesh to flinch.

Grins of triumph were pasted upon the faces of the troopers as they pumped fresh shells into the breeches of the Henry rifles. The Lieutenant looked to his left and right and saw the hatred blazing in the eyes above the bared teeth. As the final fusillade rang out, and Forrest barked an order to halt further futile shooting, the young officer realised the men were in Union blue by an accident of geography; that not even a Southern slavemaster could have poured bullets into the blacks with as much venomous enjoyment as these soldiers.

"You can only kill a man once," he said, his voice strident with shock.

Forrest spat over the balcony rail. "With some men, we like to be sure," he growled.

"You sure yet, Forrest?" Hedges called from below.

The sergeant glanced across at the sprawled and crumpled

bodies which were the sources of many rivers of blood running to the edge of the steps and sidewalk to drip into the mud. "Ain't not one of em' goin' to get up, I reckon, Captain," he said.

Hedges stepped into view, clothed only in his grey underwear. Seward started a snigger, but silenced it under the hard-eyed stare. He confined his amusement to the same style of silent grin as the other troopers when the Captain turned his back to look out into the street.

"Rhett!"

The New Englander raised his head from out of his hastily dug hole. "I did like you said, sir," he whined. "You want me to get your uniform off him?"

"A live one'd be more fun, Bob," Scott called.

It provided all the troopers with an opportunity to vent their amusement at the scantily-clad Captain while pretending that Rhett was the butt.

"I want you to get seven uniforms!" Hedges barked, and the laughter suddenly trailed away. "Grey ones."

"What the hell?" Forrest exploded.

Hedges whirled around and raked his slitted eyes along the row of faces staring down at him. "You got it, sergeant!" he snarled, fixing his gaze upon the mean set features of Forrest. "We're goin' to do what General Grant wants."

The Lieutenant whistled a sigh of relief. With Marlowe and the hotel clerk – an undercover man for the Pinkerton agency – both dead, he would have been alone in facing official ire if the mission had failed.

Rhett had hauled himself to his feet and was looking up at Forrest. A flicker of the sergeant's eyes revealed to Hedges that the man behind him was waiting for the order to be given approval by the non-com.

"Move it, trooper!" the Captain snapped, not turning around. "Or I'll kill you."

The slivers of his eyes dared Forrest to intercede before Rhett started forward. Both the Captain and the sergeant held a rifle and for several stretched seconds all the watchers knew both were ready to raise and fire the weapons. Even the shavetail, for whom such a showdown situation between a non-com and an officer was an utterly new experience was alert. The troopers had been witnesses to many similar unmilitary stand-offs.

"They'll have holes and be covered with blood," Rhett pointed out nervously, still looking to Forrest for a sign.

"Three seconds and you'll know the feeling," Hedges said softly.

Mud made a moist sound as Rhett lifted a boot from the quagmire. A harsh laugh erupted from Forrest, splitting his thin mouth wide and draining the tension from his body. He tore his eyes from the trap of Hedges' stare and looked along the row of faces.

"Be like the old days," he said easily as the laugh ended. "Goin' after just the one man. Like a bounty hunt."

The Lieutenant nodded enthusiastically. "If you get him, it could end the war. That would be the biggest bounty in history."

"Lucky the niggers turned mean now instead of later," Forrest growled.

Hedges allowed the forbidden epithet to pass, recognising its use as a balm to the sergeant's wounded ego.

"We'd have still blasted 'em good, Frank," Seward boasted.

"Sure," Forrest agreed as he watched Hedges turn to re-enter the hotel lobby. "But we wouldn't want a mutiny on the bounty hunt."

The masked men remained cool in the hot sun beating down upon the birthday celebrations which had turned sour. After the thin man had heaved the bag of money up on to the roof, the masked man with the shotgun stepped forward and picked it up. He didn't open it. Instead, he whirled and moved to the side of the building. It was an easy jump for him. Because of the angle of the corner, he was out of sight for a few moments. When he reappeared, he was astride a white horse. The money bag was hung from the saddle, its handles hooked over the horn. One of his hands held the bridle of the piebald mare he was leading. The other held his own reins as well as being curled around the shotgun, the stock of which was nestled in his armpit.

"My buddy's going to jump now, folks," he announced. "Be out of sight for awhile. But he'll be seeing me. And he'll sure enough hear a shot. He does, you'll hear a shot. Sheriff's wife'll hear it louder."

"Don't anybody try anything!" the ashen-faced lawman ordered, swinging around to show his determination to the whole assembly. His final stare was at Edge.

The tall half-breed shrugged. "I'm a patient man, Sheriff," he said.

"You better have a lot of it, mister," the man with the shotgun rapped out, recapturing every pair of eyes. "That goes for all of you. We intend to take the lady a mile outa town before we let her go. We have to ditch her before that, bring out some shovels as well as your guns. You get my drift.?"

His eyes above the neckerchief mask met and locked with the Sheriff's. Pitman nodded. "We get it."

The woman gave a yell of alarm as she was forced to jump from the roof, still in the clutches of the second masked man. The sound changed to one of pain. Pitman made to move forward, but the slight lift of the shotgun's barrels froze him.

"Sprained ankle, is all," her captor announced as he emerged from the angle of the wall, one arm still wrapped around the petrified woman as the other hand pressed the revolver against her head.

There was a fraction of a second, as he slung the woman across the horse and then swung up into the saddle, when it would have been possible to put a bullet into him before he could fire the revolver. But only one man in the crowd would have been prepared to take the chance. Like so many before him, the masked man with the shotgun sensed the mark of the killer in the lean features of the half-breed and it was at Edge that the shotgun pointed during that vital iota of time. The Winchester stayed resting easily against the deceptively lean shoulder.

"Thanks for everything folks," the spokesman for the two said brightly. "Just remember to hold still until we drop off the lady. Then do what you have to."

The man with the lawman's wife across his horse started out first, thudding in his heels to demand a gallop. His partner allowed him a start of a few yards, then wheeled his horse and raced in pursuit. Grazing cattle raised their heads to the sound of the thudding hoofbeats, then resumed feeding. The un-conscious Jefferson groaned his way back to awareness.

Like the others in the crowd, Edge watched in unmoving silence as the dust cloud blurring the forms of horses and riders receded into the distance. He watched as the hold-up men reined their horses to a halt. The dust did not have time to settle until they lunged forward into a gallop again. The woman emerged from the yellow cloud, staggering back towards town in a limp-ing run. Her husband gave a grunt of anguish and barged through the crowd, racing out along the trail to meet her. A hub-bub of conversation broke out among the crowd.

Edge continued to watch the departing hold-up men, follow-ing their progress as they angled off the trail and cut across the open range to go from sight around the hump of a hill. Then he whirled, stepped down from the sidewalk and strode quickly along the street towards the livery. He sensed the eyes of the thin man on him, but did not glance across to the front of the law office where he had been standing since tossing the bag of money up to the men.

The liveryman was not at the stable and had not put in an appearance by the time Edge had saddled the gelding. There was a neatly printed scale of charges tacked to the inside of the door and he peeled off enough bills from his shrinking bankroll to cover his debt. There was a paperknife on the battered desk and he used it to spear the bills to the half door of the stall which the gelding had occupied. Then he mounted and rode out into the diminished heat of the sun as afternoon gave evening a pale yellow kiss.

There was no longer any breeze and the street decorations hung limply, sadly – as if in sympathy with the mood of the people below. The crowd was dispersing, only a few waiting to watch as Sheriff Pitman helped his wife back along the trail.

The old barber was as melancholic as everybody else. He was one of those drifting away from the area of the prizefight, where Jefferson and the thin man were dismantling the ring.

"Who died?" Edge asked.

The old-timer shook his head. "Not who. What. A tradition, stranger. We ain't never had no trouble in Jerusalem. For better than ten years. First there was what you done to the sheriff last afternoon. Now what's happened today."

"Real tough," Edge said sardonically, clucking his mount forward. "Maybe you ought to build a wailing wall."

The barber was confused. Then he shrugged and continued on his way to the shop. Edge rode slowly along the street to where Jefferson and the thin man were loading the ropes and posts of the ring on to the back of a buckboard. McNally was nowhere in sight. The thin man looked up, startled, as Edge's shadow fell across him. His fear expanded as he saw the familiar icy glint in the narrowed eyes. He nudged Jefferson, who donned his toughest expression.

"You want something?" the beefy young fighter rasped.

"Twenty-two grand," Edge replied easily.

"You saw what happened to the money!" the thin man whined.

Edge nodded. "I saw."

"Everythin' I got is in that bag," the thin man pleaded. "I can't pay you."

The sheriff and his wife were still a half mile out on the trail. The waiters – mostly citizens of Jerusalem and the owners of the farmsteads in the immediate vicinity – turned their attention to the drama closer at hand. The thin man looked around at them imploringly.

"What can I do?"

Several heads shook and some shoulders were shrugged. Edge guessed that all the money except his had been riding on Jefferson.

"You can hope," the half-breed advised, and curled back his thin lips to show a cruel grin as the thin man blinked at him in perplexity. "That there's more than twenty-two grand in the bag, feller," he explained.

"More?" Jefferson snarled.

Edge nodded. "The balance I take for my trouble."

The prizefighter seemed intent upon arguing the point, but the thin man nodded.

"Sure. Sure, mister. You catch up with them, you'll have earned it."

"Obliged," Edge said wryly, then wiped the grin from his lean features. His voice became a rasping whisper. "And if I find out I've been cheated of my due, I'll find you and take the balance from your hide."

The thin man swallowed hard, unable to speak. Jefferson was ready to step into the breach, but the older man laid a restraining hand on his shoulder. "Don't mess with him," he warned.

The crowd parted to allow Edge to ride through and he did not rein his horse again until he reached the very end of the street. The fat lawman and his hobbling wife glared up at the rider hatefully.

"I already heard," Edge told them. "First me, then the stick-up. Things around here are still green, but they ain't so pleasant no more."

Pitman held the venom in his eyes, but kept his voice flat, un-threatening. "Just ride on out like you said, mister. And don't come back."

"No sweat, sheriff," Edge replied, swinging his horse to the side to go around the couple. "I'm owed. And I ain't gonna get those kinda dues in Jerusalem."

CHAPTER FIVE ·

The men needed sleep and the hotel in Hartford Gap contained ample beds for them. But they complied willingly with Hedges' order to move out of the town as soon as they were all attired in stolen uniforms marking them as enlisted men in the Second Kentucky Infantry.

As Rhett had predicted, the grey clothes were caked with mud and showed red stains around ominous holes. And, because of the mutilating effect of the mill explosion, the choice was limited to a selection of those clothes on the Rebels killed during the gun battle. Only Douglas got a tunic and pair of pants which came close to being a good fit. The others, clustered in a group outside the hotel, were quite obviously dressed in hand-me-downs. All were armed with Spencer rifles.

"Good luck, sir," the Lieutenant said, throwing up a copy-book salute. "It won't be easy."

"What is, in this friggin' war?" Seward muttered acidly.

Hedges responded to the salute by touching the peak of his ill-fitting forage cap, then turned to the men. "Move out. It's a long walk to Richmond."

All the horses which had survived the deadly cross-fire from the roof-tops had bolted and none had returned to the scene of its panic.

The troopers formed into a single file and started to trudge wearily through the clinging mud, leaving behind the dead men sprawled on the sidewalks and under the wagons, heading for the dismembered bodies scattered over the intersection. None gave a thought to the corpses, except as vivid examples of what could well happen to themselves if the shavetail's presumption was correct. For, as the Lieutenant had said, there had been two civilians remaining in Hartford Gap when the Federal forces took the town. Both were supposed to be undercover men for the Pinkerton Agency. One was now spread-eagled in the mud. The other had disappeared an hour before the wagon train was ambushed and it could well be the missing man who had informed to the Rebels.

This possibility, coupled with the chance that there were more Rebels in the area, waiting for Major Collins and his men to return, was why the Union troopers had given Hedges no argument when he ordered them to move out.

"Where's buddy-boy goin'?" Forrest asked when the men had angled across the intersection and were heading east on the cross street under a sky that still looked like a black sponge waiting for another squeeze.

Hedges tugged at the crotch of his tight-fitting pants. "I got enough problems, *sergeant*," he replied, putting stress on the rank.

Forrest got the message. "You didn't ask him, *sir*?"

"He might have told me, and then I might have worried about him," Hedges replied sourly.

They moved across the eastern limits of town and the pale moonlight showed the trail ahead winding through rolling farmland. But Virginia had suffered perhaps more than any other state from the ravages of war. It had been a long time since many of the fields had been tilled and for the most part they were overgrown with crops gone wild and choked by weeds. Only a few of the farmsteads showed signs of recent habitation. The others had fallen into various states of disrepair. Some sagging timbers bore the scars of war in the shape of bullet holes. Here and there, blackened frameworks were outlined against the night – the remains of buildings put to the torch.

But the going was easier in open country, for the men were able to move off the bog-like trail and tramp across fields. The surface was spongy after the heavy rain, but living roots held the soil together and kept it from breaking down into mud.

The fact that he was leading the men across farmland, and his sardonic reference to worry about the young Lieutenant, caused Hedges to think of Jamie. His crippled brother ought to be safe enough, secure in Iowa far from the battle grounds. He ought to be taking care of the farm without too many problems, aided by the money Hedges sent to him whenever he was able. But Jamie was young and he was alone. And he had a bum leg. It was natural to worry about him, Hedges reasoned: and he had a lot of anxiety to spare. For the long, bloody years of war had forged a new set of values for the Captain. Survival and the protection of what one cared about were all that mattered. Josiah C. Hedges cared about himself and his brother.

"What made you agree to blast Jeff Davis?" Forrest said suddenly. He added: "Sir?"

They had covered perhaps three miles and Hartford Gap was lost to sight through the night and behind intervening hills. Hedges had not been lost in thought. His hooded eyes had been constantly alert, flicking to left and right then straight ahead: searching for a sign of trouble. But the sergeant's remark startled him. Not for the first time, Forrest was revealing that he possessed a useful attribute for a professional killer. He could not read another man's mind, but he did have a kind of perceptive sense that gave him a clue to a secret train of thought. The sort of talent which, in a gunfight showdown, would tell him a fraction of a second before a move what action his opponent was going to take. Or perhaps Forrest was just a guesser – a right one, since he was still alive.

"To end it," Hedges replied after a pause, not turning as he continued to survey the terrain ahead. "I was stretched out on the floor in that crumby hotel. Stripped to my underwear with mud all over my face and flour in my eyes. Getting ready to blast guys supposed to be on my side – before they blasted me. And I suddenly thought about my spread in Iowa. I knew where I'd rather be. Putting some bullets in Davis might just get me back home a lot sooner than making cavalry charges against Reb artillery barrages."

"And maybe put up your life expectancy?" Forrest asked slyly.

Hedges halted abruptly and whirled. Forrest stopped suddenly and reached for a gun holster that wasn't there. He cursed, then again as the unfortunate Bell collided with him. Bell, with

the other troopers, backed away. The prospect of trouble between the officer and the sergeant drove the weariness from their
red-rimmed eyes. Forrest made a move to bring up his rifle, but
halted it when he saw Hedges' Spencer was still held low in
front and across him. Each surveyed the other's unflinching features across a distance of three feet. Forrest's narrowed eyes
were challenging. He made wet sounds with his tongue against
the roof of his mouth. Hedges' eyes were as impassive as the rest
of his features.

"You calling me a name, sergeant?" he asked softly.

Forrest sniffed and it was wetter than the sound from his
mouth. "I might be saying I ain't sure . . . sir."

"What's this all about, Frank?" Billy Seward wanted to know.

The sergeant ignored the question, watching and waiting for
Hedges' reaction to the barb.

"I think Frank's accusing the Captain of being like Bob,
Billy," John Scott attempted to explain.

"You mean like queer?" Seward exclaimed, shocked.

"He means like yellow," Hedges muttered.

Rhett scowled at the first comment. "I do my best," he answered to the second, but nobody was listening to him.

"I mean you suddenly got mighty careful lately " Forrest
corrected. "You got caught in the open when the Rebs hit. But
both times *you* made the crap fly back there, you was tucked up
nice and safe behind solid walls."

"Hey, that's right!" Rhett put into the tense silence, siezing
upon an opportunity to redeem himself. "It was me he sent out
into the open without a weapon to defend myself with."

"Bob?" Hal Douglas said.

"Yeah?"

"If I was down to my underwear, I'd send you outside."

Rhett groaned his frustration and nobody laughed.

"Well, Captain?" Forrest demanded, his mouth line twisting
into a sneer.

All the troopers stared intently into the hard set lines of Hedges' face. He swung his gaze away from the expectant face of
Forrest and raked the features of the others. His eyes betrayed
nothing of what he was feeling or thinking. But in his stance,

with feet slightly apart, weight evenly balanced and body canted almost imperceptibly forward, there was a latent threat which caused each man to take a tighter grip on his Spencer.

"You others agree with Forrest and Rhett?" he asked softly.

"Between you and me, Hedges!" the sergeant snarled as the troopers shuffled back under the pressure of the flat-eyed stare and quiet strength of the voice. "The boys are with me, but I don't need 'em to help me take you."

"Take him good, Frank!" Seward urged with a giggle, careful not to look at Hedges in case he was trapped by the killer's stare.

"We've both known for a long time this was gonna happen," Forrest rasped.

Hedges gave a short nod of agreement. "Make your move," he said simply.

A laugh rasped from the sneering mouth of the sergeant, as if the humour had substance and his throat was lined with sand-paper. "You calling me, kid?" he taunted. "I had the rep as the fastest man with a gun in the entire south-west."

"Hope you haven't lost the talent," Hedges replied easily.

Forrest blinked, which could have been fatal had Hedges been so inclined. "Uh?"

Hedges pursed his lips. "You're gonna have to be real fast, sergeant. First to blast me before I put a bullet between your eyes and maybe even hit your pea-size brain." The anger expanded from the mean eyes to spread colourfully across the entire dirt-streaked surface of Forrest's face. It reached his hands too late. He had moved the Spencer only a fraction of an inch before he was forced to freeze. Hedges did not only swing his rifle from the hip. He snapped it up to his shoulder and drew a bead with the gun muzzle no more than in inch away from the sparse flesh of Forrest's forehead. "Then you gotta be real fast on your legs," Hedges went on in the same low tones. "To get the hell out of here after that bunch of soldiers on the road come looking for – "

"Jesus, there's a hundred of 'em!"

All the troopers except the two men facing each other had whirled at Hedges' warning. It was Rhett who exploded the croaky exclamation, hurling himself to the ground. The others

68

were just a moment behind him in hitting the deck. Sweat showed on the area of forehead threatened by the rifle muzzle. It oozed from distended pores and pressured through the grime of dirt. There was a soft thud as the sergeant's rifle slid from his opened palms and hit the sodden ground.

"You're faster," he allowed without grace. "And your timing is a hell of a lot better."

"And I've got a hell of a lot more careful lately," Hedges muttered, backing away from the sergeant, lowering the Spencer and dropping into a crouch.

Forrest went down, turning as he did so, to look at the Confederate soldiers on the trail. He wiped the back of his hand across his mouth and when the move was complete, his lips parted to show his tobacco-stained teeth in a wry grin. "They wouldn't have seen us," he whispered. "But, I gotta admit, a shot would have brung 'em running."

Ever since Hedges first saw the Rebels, when he looked at the troopers to ask if they were backing Forrest, he had been sure he and his men were safe from being seen. For the enemy – Rhett's estimate of a hundred was about right – were struggling through the mud of the trail. Their pace was dictated by the crawl at which a half-dozen horses were able to drag as many artillery pieces. They were coming from the direction of Hartford Gap and were still better than a half-mile from where the Union troopers crouched and sprawled on the ground. But it was not only the distance which protected the troopers. The spot where Forrest had chosen to make his play was under the brow of a rise, the crest of which was shrouded in timber. Thus, apart from being dark shapes against a dark background of hillside, the troopers were also in the deep shadow of the tree clump.

"Back," Hedges said softly and the men covered the remaining few yards of open ground to reach the even greater security of the trees themselves. A nod from the Captain told Forrest he could pick up his discarded rifle on the way.

Once more, the proximity of the enemy caused the mean-faced sergeant to set aside his enmity towards Hedges and it was as if this latest of several such incidents had never happened.

"Looks like they come through town," Forrest said, crouching down beside the officer between the massive trunks of two oak trees.

"And through a battle before that," Hedges answered, raking his hooded eyes along the straggling line of soldiers as the column drew closer.

In the comparative safety of the wood, the troopers were able to view the Rebels with objectivity — to see beyond the simple fact that the men were an enemy to be feared. And, like Hedges, they saw that many of the men below were walking wounded. Although stained by weather and sweat, bandages around heads and limbs still showed up pale against the mud-spattered uniforms of the soldiers. Some of the men hobbled along with the aid of makeshift crutches while others leaned on their comrades for support.

"Hell, only half of 'em are still in one piece," Seward whispered excitedly. "What say we take a few potshots at 'em?"

"Sure, Billy!" Hal Douglas agreed. "They got no cover down there and they ain't gonna be able to run away very damn fast."

Hedges merely looked at Forrest with one eyebrow raised and his lips slightly parted in a sneer of scorn. The sergeant, returned to his status as an understanding second-in-command, gave a slight nod.

"Billy? Hal?"

"Yeah, Frank?" Seward acknowledged with his excitement still high.

Forrest spat through the gorse brushing his face. "You make any more half-ass suggestions like that, I'm gonna put bullets in both your butts. Then you'll see how fast those guys down there can move. And when those cannon start lobbing shells up here, I reckon you two might get kinda athletic.'

Seward and Douglas scowled at each other.

The trail angled across the foot of the hill from which the Union troopers were watching, then curved to snake around it. Less than three hundred yards separated the observed and the observers at the point where they were closest and it was then that Hedges saw a blue uniform among the grey. The sergeant saw it, too.

"They got the Lieutenant," Forrest said dispassionately.

The young shavetail was close to the head of the column, trudging through the mud in the wake of three officers and two artillery pieces. Behind him was a big corporal with a levelled rifle. Whenever the Lieutenant fell, the corporal hauled him roughly to his feet and pushed him forward with a jab of the rifle. The Lieutenant went down into the sludge often for his arms were lashed behind his back from pits to wrists, impairing his equilibrium.

"Wonder why they don't just leave him down to choke in the crap?" Forrest muttered coldly.

"Same reason they didn't shoot him, I guess," Hedges replied. "Let's go."

He rose and turned to move deeper into the trees capping the hill top and the men followed, sacrificing silence for speed in the knowledge that the noise caused by the progress of the Rebels provided ample cover for the sounds of swishing ferns, cracking twigs and heavy breathing.

The timber extended further down the slope on the eastern face of the hill and did not thin out until the ground fell away in an almost sheer, twenty-feet high cliff face to the very edge of the trail the Rebels were following. On the other side of the trail, a swollen river arced around the base of a rise. It had burst its bank and was lapping around a stranded stage with the nearside rear corner sunk deep into the mud as a result of a broken wheel.

Seven men in Western dress were attempting to manhandle the stage up from the grip of the mud with a singular lack of success. The four horse team were still in the traces, snorting as they struggled to get free of the same water-covered mud. Because of the angle adopted by the crippled stage, the legend painted on the side was clearly visible to the troopers peering down over the rim of the cliff:

THE JOHN FORD TOURING COMPANY
PORTRAYING THE WEST AS IT REALLY IS

"Seems the stage ain't what it used to be," Forrest whispered after watching the struggles of the men below for several moments.

"Shut up and wait for the next act," Hedges rasped, looking to left and right.

They had emerged at the highest point on the cliff. In both directions the ground fell away and he knew he had ample time to lead the men down the incline to the east and be long gone from sight before the head of the Rebel column rounded the turn in the trail and saw the way barred by the crippled stage. And the group of actors were too intent on their chore to be concerned with other things.

But Hedges remained prone on the soaking ground, setting aside his original plan which was to get ahead of the enemy soldiers and use the greater mobility of the smaller group to extend the gap. For he had the germ of a new idea, the feasibility of which depended upon what was about to happen below.

Ten minutes were lost in the damp darkness of the early hours before the Rebels rounded the obstacle of the hill and the leading officers saw the barrier across their path. The actors spotted the soldiers at the same time, for they were resting, leaning against the tilted stage to recover from an exhausting, concerted effort which had raised the burden a few inches. But when one of them had turned away to reach for a blocking rock, the others had missed his strength. The stage had settled down lower than ever.

The officers – two Captains and a Leiutenant with a bandage around his throat – were cool. They hesitated only a moment then kept coming along the trail. During the brief pause, they had drawn Colts from their holsters.

"It's okay," one of the actors said breathlessly. "Southerners." Then, when the head of the column was closer, he raised his voice. "Boy, are we glad to see you fellers!" he yelled.

The column ground to a grateful halt with less than ten feet between the officers and the actors grouped at the rear of the crippled stage.

"Are you authorised to be on this road?" the taller Captain asked. He and the other two officers held their revolvers negligently, but nonetheless pointed towards the civilians.

"Sure, Captain," the spokesman for the actors replied. "We're entertainers. We got papers sent from Richmond. Saying we can put on shows – for the army and civilians alike. Helps to keep up morale in these troubled times."

"Check them out, Lieutenant."

As the Rebel junior officer moved forward and held out his hands for the papers proffered by the acting troupe's top man, the Union shavetail sank to his knees. He twisted as he fell, and sprawled out on his back in mud. Water from the flooded river seeped into the indentation made by his body. The corporal guarding him stepped forward and inserted a boot under his head. His face stayed above the water level as the rest of him was swamped. The Union troopers looking down at him were unable to tell whether the Lieutenant was expressing pain, for his face showed too many signs of past suffering. They had beaten him until not a fraction of an inch of his features remained unmarked. His forehead, cheeks and throat were swollen by evil-coloured bruises. His eyes were sunk deep in the inflated flesh. His nose was an ugly blob of pulp crusted with dried blood. His puffed lips were slightly parted to show twin rows of broken teeth. Trickles of blood turned black by drying zig-zagged across the injuries which had been their sources.

"He looks beat," Forrest whispered, then clamped his lips tight closed as he met Hedges' icy stare.

"Papers look okay, sir," the Rebel Lieutenant reported. "Shall I check the stage?"

"Make it fast," the Captain rapped.

"You gonna give us a hand to raise her?"

"No time, mister," the Captain answered, as the Lieutenant splashed back to his place and gave a nod to indicate that the contents of the stage bore out what the papers said. "We have an important prisoner to deliver to headquarters."

The top man of the actors – a thin-faced, stooped shouldered man of about forty – grimaced. "Only take a minute. Just to get her up with some rocks under her. We'll fix the busted wheel ourselves."

"You heard me, mister!" the Captain snapped. He looked over his shoulder as he thrust his revolver back in its holster. "Move out, men!" he shouted, and splashed into the shallows of the river, leading the column around the stranded stage.

The shavetail was hauled roughly to his feet and prodded forward in the wake of the two horses and guns.

"You see seven men in Confederate infantry uniforms in this part of the country, be careful," the Captain shouted back to the angry actors. "They could be Federal spies."

"He talked!" Scott rasped disgustedly.

Forrest spat silently.

"Pained him to do it," Bell muttered.

The column waded on a curved course around the tilted stage as the actors watched miserably.

"Thought the show was always supposed to go on!" a Rebel taunted.

"If the West's like that, you can keep it," another called

A man with a bandaged knee, leaning against another with a head dressing, looked up at the sky. "Pity," he mused. "Weather's clearing. More rain and maybe she'd have floated up for you."

His companion laughed.

Not until the tail of the column had passed, did the actors return their attention to the stage, straining and cursing in their struggles. Hedges looked away from them, peering along the trail towards the east and watching as the Rebel soldiers diminished into the distance: then were lost to sight in an area of wooded country. The sky above the woods had taken on a definite lighter shade – the first sign of a new dawn in the offing.

He peered downwards again and gave a nod as he reached his decision.

"What now?" Forrest whispered.

"Curtains for the actors," Hedges replied. "But no applause. Real quiet."

Forrest glanced over the top of the cliff. "That way?"

"I reckon."

"We could all break something."

Hedges' teeth showed in a cold grin. "You scared, sergeant?"

Forrest paused, then matched the Captain's expression. He shook his head. "Just happy you stopped being careful." He swung around to look at the troopers. "You all in the picture?"

They responded with apprehensive nods, glancing at the depth of the drop they had to make. Forrest drew a knife and the others followed his example. Hedges reached up to the back of his neck. The open razor came free of the pouch. The others took their lead from the Captain in standing, blade in one hand and rifle in the other. They eased forward to the edge of the cliff.

"Let's drop by the show!" Hedges rasped, and launched forward.

With the exception of Rhett, the troopers were only a moment behind the Captain. The actors were in the middle of a renewed effort to raise the stage, straining with all their might as they prised the unwieldly burden clear of the sucking sludge. They were completely unaware of the attack until the six Union men thudded down into the mud, sending up great sprays of black water. One of the actors cried in alarm and tried to back away. But he slipped, his feet and legs shooting in front of him. The others released their grip on the stage and the enormous weight fell back to rest. The man who had slipped was crushed between the buckled wheel rim and the submerged rock that had caused the damage. His groan of agony was curtailed as his stomach burst open and exploded soggy pieces of red meat through the muddy water.

Then the troopers were lunging at the terrified actors, throwing their feet high to make speed through the quagmire

Seward reached his man first, hooking one arm around his neck and using the actor's rigidity to power himself the final foot of the way. The knife went underhand into the actor's belly and the grinning Seward clamped a hand over the gaping mouth to stop the scream. The man went backwards, taking himself off the skewer of the knife. Seward went down with him and held the head under the slimy water until the bubbles ceased to rise.

Forrest went for a stab to the belly, also. But with his greater strength, he was able to jerk the knife upwards, ripping open the man's body from navel to chest. "Just wanted to see what you were made of," he rasped into the death mask of agony.

The man before Hedges started to turn, as if to run away. The Captain's right arm moved up and across in a speed blur. It was the long arm of a tall man. He stabbed with the razor and the blade sank an inch into the flesh below his victim's right ear.

Hedges turned his wrist and his action became slashing. A great wake of blood was thrown up behind the course of the razor ploughing across the throat. The blade came free under the left ear.

"Lousy death scene," he muttered as the actor crumpled without a sound.

Scott and Bell discovered they had both chosen the same man. Scott went for the heart and Bell for the stomach. The man was pressed against the rear of the stage. Both knives sank in to the hilts. The blood didn't start until they withdrew the blades. Then it poured in torrents. The two killers grinned at each other. Then fear leapt into Bell's eyes and he suddenly hurled his blood-coated knife. It spun over Scott's shoulder and sliced deep into the blazing right eye of a man holding a large rock above his head.

Scott whirled and watched the man collapse, smashing the rock into his own dead face. "Saved by the Bell!" he gasped.

Douglas was straddling his victim, who he had knocked down with a superficial stab wound in the chest, blocked by a rib bone. Now the corporal was flailing wildly at the actor with the dripping knife as the man bucked and moaned beneath him. The other troopers had made their kills within the space of a few seconds. They watched dispassionately as the surviving actor suffered terribly at Douglas' butchery.

"He won't die!" the attacker shrieked as he plunged in the knife again, withdrew it and stabbed.

"Real tough cat," Seward muttered. Stab.

"Got nine lives," Scott put in. Stab.

Hedges lunged forward, sank to his knees and slashed open the throat of the victim. The moans became a final sigh and the struggling ceased. Tears of frustration gleamed in Douglas' eyes as he met the icy stare of the Captain.

"He wouldn't die!" Douglas pleaded again.

Hedges got to his feet and trudged across to recover his rifle. "Corporal punishment never killed anyone," he answered, and glanced up towards the top of the cliff.

Rhett's face was very white against the background of the trees

76

"I was covering you, Captain!" the New Englander called down, his voice high-pitched and quivering.

"Obliged," Hedges said wryly, and spat into the mud, then wiped the blade of the razor on his pants leg. "But you can come down now."

"Jump?"

"A fairy ought to know how to fly," Forrest snarled. "Yeah, jump you yellow bastard."

Rhett groaned, took a deep breath and launched himself into mid-air. He sent up a great gout of mud and water as he landed. He stayed on his feet and grinned in triumph at the achievement. "How about that?" he announced gleefully.

"You always were good for a jump, Bob," Roger Bell drawled.

The trail of the two hold-up men led Edge in a wide half circle around the western rim of the verdant valley at the centre of which was the town of Jerusalem. At first, it was easy for the slitted eyes of the tall half-breed to see the sign left by riders and horses. But then day drew to a close and the period of twilight was short

The half-moon was bright and there were no cloud patches to veil it. But it hung low in the sky, spreading deep shadows through the timber and – higher up in the Big Horn Mountains – dropping solid pools of darkness among the rugged rock formations. Night, in collaboration with firmer ground which was less inclined to show sign of his quarries' passing, slowed the progress of the solitary rider.

But after awhile, a pattern emerged. The wide swing around Jerusalem ended short of the trail from the south. The hold-up men had turned west, climbing every yard of the way, then at the crest line of the first step of the range had veered northwards. Edge followed the easiest course and at infrequent intervals saw horse droppings, cigarette butts and hoofprints in pockets of soft earth.

When he reached the barrier of a rearing slab of solid rock, he elected to follow a narrow gully that canted steeply up towards the star-dotted western sky. At the top, it levelled off and then opened out on a high plateau. A trail bisected the rocky flatland and at

the very centre was a small group of frame buildings. They looked distant and desolate in the pale moonglow. The shout reached
Edge like the last of many echoes down a long valley. A stage
emerged from among the buildings, pulled by a six horse team
whipped into a gallop, heading north. The clatter of hoofbeats
reached him late and distorted.

He watched for a few moments, lean face impassive as he considered the alternatives. Then he thudded in his heels and jerked
on the reins, urging the gelding into a gallop towards the buildings. As he drew closer, he saw they formed a stage line way station. The largest building was the office and waiting room. One
of its windows was lit. The others were stables, a feed barn and
a shack for the company man to live in.

Edge rode in among the buildings at a casual walk, carefully
but not furtively. Two horses were hitched to the rail outside
the main building. He had last seen the animals raising dust on
the trail out of Jerusalem. Also familiar was the sign hung on the
front of the single storey building: WYOMING–MONTANA–
COLORADO LINE. Like the rest of the station, the sign was in
a better state of repair than the old line shack south of Jerusalem.

The half-breed angled his horse across to the hitching rail and
maintained an attitude of calm self-assurance as he slid from the
saddle and tethered the gelding. He had his back to the doorway
as he stooped to check the tension of the cinch. But he heard the
creak of the opening door, and the wedge of light it spilled fell
across him.

"Stage has left, mister," a man announced, his voice scratchy
with age. "Not another until next week."

Edge sensed there was more than just the one man behind him.
He straightened slowly, then whirled, drawing on the pivot. The
company man was older than his voice. He was short and thin
and looked ready to fall over if anybody breathed too heavily on
him. More than eighty hard years had carved a network of lines
deep into the slack flesh clinging to the angular bones of his face.
His yellow tinged eyes seemed to be dead already. His hair had
given up and fallen out long ago. His slack mouth twitched
violently when he saw the Colt in the brown hand of the half-
breed.

78

"Jesus, mister, ain't nothing here worth the stealing!" he pleaded.

"What I want's already been stole," Edge said, directing his voice and his hooded-eyed stare over the top of the old-timer's head at the two tall men standing behind him.

The neckerchief masks they had worn during the hold-up had been no disguise at all. They were obviously the same pair of good looking youngsters in their early twenties. Their clothes were the same, except that they had removed their hats. This emphasized the distinctive auburn and blond of their hair. Only the eyes were different, this because of a change of expression. In Jerusalem the two pairs of brown eyes had shown nervousness. Now, as they looked from the gun in Edge's hand up to his unrelenting stare, naked fear distended the irises.

"I told you it was him," the blond whispered hoarsely to his partner.

The redhead recovered first and made a fast draw. A gasp from the old-timer and a slight bowing of his emaciated body told where the revolver had been jabbed. "Drop the iron, or old man Fargo gets lead in his spine," the man ordered calmly.

Edge did not even blink and his gun hand remained rock steady, the revolver's muzzle aimed over the naked skull of the old timer, between the heads of the two youngsters. The blond looked at the redhead as if he couldn't believe what he had heard.

"Clint!" he gasped.

"Please, mister!" the old-timer begged.

"He ain't nothing to me," Edge said. "You kill him, I got more of you to aim at, feller."

"Please?" Fargo tried again, his voice rising in pitch. "This ain't my fight."

"Let me explain," the blond implored.

"He don't look like a good listener," Aaron," Clint said, his tone still tough. His eyes suggested the statement could be a question.

"Money talks," Edge replied evenly. "I've got twenty thousand good reasons to listen if you say the right words, feller."

"Twenty thousand!" Aaron exclaimed, and beads of sweat broke out on his forehead. "Christ, Clint."

The announcement hit Clint hard, too. But he handled it better. A lump rose to his throat. It bobbed and he swallowed it. "There wasn't that much in the bag," he argued.

Edge nodded. "That figures. The difference is between me and the guy who took my bet. It could be the difference between life and death for him."

"You threatening us, mister?" Clint snapped.

Fargo controlled the trembling of his slack mouth. "He ain't the kind of man to make the idle kind," he said knowledgeably. "I seen lots like him."

"Get your buddy to toss out the money bag," Edge ordered, tightening his voice and ignoring the old-timer.

"Fat chance," Clint snarled. "You don't scare me."

The Colt bucked in Edge's hand. The three horses snorted at the sound and jerked back. But the rail held them prisoner. Clint remained on his feet for long seconds, blood from a hole in the centre of his forehead streaming out to splash on the bald dome of the old-timer. Fargo shuddered at the touch of the warm stickiness, then slumped into a faint. Clint went down at the same time, his surprised eyes snapping closed and the gun slipping from his lifeless fingers.

"You killed my brother!" Aaron screamed, finding his voice at the end of a brief period of dumb shock. "You killed Clint!"

"He died rich," Edge muttered. "I figure I inherit."

"You bastard!" Aaron shouted. "Just like that, you killed him. We didn't want no trouble. It was just that we wanted to help – "

Edge's glittering slits of eyes drove back the mounting hysteria and Aaron halted in mid-sentence. "You want to pass me out the money now, feller?" he asked softly, ducking under the rail but keeping the revolver aimed directly at the white-faced youngster.

"All right! I'll get it."

Aaron stepped back into the doorway and reached to the side. When his body swayed upright again, his holster was empty. The revolver he had used to press against the temple of the sheriff's wife was now aimed at Edge. He fired from the hip and he wasn't that good with a gun. Edge dropped into a crouch and heard one

80

of the horses snort with pain. The animal thudded to the ground as the other two tried again to wrench free from the rail.

"You get it!" Edge hissed, and the Colt exploded a second time.

The bullet drilled into Aaron's heart and he fell like a tree, stiff and straight. The blood bubbled up from the ragged hole and expanded an ugly dark stain over his shirt front. Edge slid the gun back into its holster and stepped over the two dead brothers and the senseless Fargo. He cast a quick glance around the room. It was large, sparsely and crudely furnished with a bureau and a table surrounded by a half dozen chairs. The men had been seated at the table, drinking coffee, when Edge's approach disturbed them. The coffee pot was half full and still warm to the touch. Edge emptied one cup on the floor and refilled it. The coffee was lukewarm and weak. But he finished it, listening to the groans from the old timer as he regained consciousness. The hats of the dead men hung from hooks in a wall. The shotgun rested on the floor below. Edge broke open the gun and saw it had been reloaded. He ejected both charges and dropped them in the coffee pot. After another glance around the room to check that the money bag was not there, he stepped outside.

Fargo was sitting up, rubbing the blood from his head with his shirt cuff. He looked up fearfully at the tall half-breed. "They're both dead?" he asked.

"Some folks say things happen in threes," Edge replied easily.

"You wouldn't shoot down a poor old man?" His tone was incredulous, but his eyes gave the lie to the sentiment.

Edge curled back his lips into a cold grin. "Poor? With a name like Fargo?"

"Not that Fargo," the old-timer corrected, getting shakily to his feet and leaning wearily against the doorframe. "That's young Gideon, my lousy nephew. He's with the lousy Government, so he's got pull. Fixed every line I've tried to operate. Him and Butterfield. Even registered the name Wells Fargo so me and my partner couldn't use it. Jim Wells has pulled out. But I don't give up that easy. I'll show young Gideon, government pull or no."

"We all got problems," Edge said. "What did those guys do with a bag they brought here?"

Fargo shrugged his thin shoulders, his eyes fearful again now that the more pressing problem of staying alive was once more of greater importance than business concerns. "I didn't see no bag, mister."

Edge leaned against the hitching rail and stroked the nose of the gelding, his hands gentle as they soothed away the skittishness caused by the gunshots and the mixed smells of blood and burnt powder. "What did you see?" he asked.

"I had just the one passenger to board here," Fargo replied quickly, anxious to be of help; fearful of the consequences if his assistance fell short of what was expected. "Little blonde girl. Mighty pretty. Rode into the station maybe an hour before the stage was due. Kinda nervous, she was. Like she was waiting for something — not just the stage, I mean. But then she sees these two fellers riding in from the hills and she's okay. They talked a lot outside here. I didn't hear nothing. And I didn't see if a bag was give to her. Stage come. One of these fellers tied her horse to the back and she got aboard. I had some coffee on the stove. We was drinking it when you showed up. The two fellers was happy. Like the girl when they come. Seeing them like that, hard to think how happy they was."

"Those folks that say things happen in threes," Edge said as he ducked under the rail and unhitched the reins.

"Yeah?"

"They also say money can't buy happiness," Edge replied, swinging up into the saddle.

The old-timer swallowed hard. "They right both times?" he asked.

"Nobody's right all the time. That girl?"

"Yeah?"

"Where'd she buy a ticket to?"

The thin shoulders shrugged. "Dunno, mister. On my line, passengers pay the driver. One thing, though."

"Yeah?"

"I seen her before. She got off the stage yesterday. Had her

82

horse tagged on behind. Untied him and rode off east, towards Jerusalem."

"She sit down while she was waiting?"

The old man blinked. "Funny kinda question, mister. Matter of fact, she didn't. Did a lot of pacing. Why?"

"Long story with a painful end," Edge told him. "Obliged for your help, Mr. Fargo," He touched his hat as he backed the gelding away from the rail with its one live and one dead horse still tied there.

"What shall I do about these fellers?" the old-timer called, suddenly nervous again.

"Bury 'em," Edge replied.

"What if somebody comes around asking questions?"

Edge nudged the gelding forward. "Say you had to bury 'em to keep 'em from smelling up the place."

Fargo sighed, aware he could expect nothing more from the tall, cold-eyed killer riding away from the station. But suddenly a thought occurred to him. "Dead men ought to have words spoke over them!" he called. "You know what to say, mister?"

"Just the one word," Edge called back without turning around.

"What's that?"

"Goodbye," Edge shouted, and urged the gelding into a gallop.

CHAPTER SIX

First the troopers heaved the bodies of the actors into the swollen river. They didn't wait to see the corpses caught by the swift current and swirled out of sight. Instead, they applied themselves to the task of man-handling the rear of the stage clear of the mud and blocking it with rocks. The wheel rim was buckled beyond repair and several spokes were broken. But there was a spare lashed to the underside of the stage. Dawn was fully broken by the time the damaged wheel had been removed, a new one fitted and the stage was rocked clear of the worst of the flooded morass and hauled along the trail on to higher and firmer ground.

The sky was a slick, grey colour and shed a grim light that emphasized the unhealthy pallor and dullness in the eyes of the men. Hedges recognized the signs of exhaustion and felt the bone-deep fatigue attacking his own body. It would have been easy to order the troopers to break out the tents stowed in the stage and make a hasty camp. But the place was wrong. Open and too close to where a Rebel patrol might stumble on the washed up bodies of the murdered actors.

"Check the trunks for clothing," the Captain ordered.

It was greeted with scowls, but no man voiced his discontent. The long haul with the wagons, the tensions of the ambush at Hartford Gap, the near showdown between Hedges and Forrest and the nervous excitement of the murders combined to drain the men of even the will to gripe. It was a dangerous state for them to be in for if they lacked what it took to argue with their own hated officer, what would be their reaction if the enemy suddenly appeared?

Turn and run? As Hedges watched Scott and Bell haul out a bulky wooden trunk while the other four leaned indifferently against the stage, he knew this was a distinct possibility. Not from cowardice, except in the case of Rhett. But from depression, triggered by exhaustion. The men had fought no part of the war with the spur of justice, patriotism or the ultimate glory of triumph to support their morale. They had donned uniforms only because this enabled them to indulge their enjoyment of killing without fear of the law's retribution. But could not even homicidal maniacs suffer from a surfeit of slaughter? Did they reach a point when the mere act of shooting or stabbing a man was not enough?

As Hedges selected a highly decorated Western outfit for himself and stripped off the blood and mud stained uniform he acknowledged that this could be so. He was his own example, although he baulked at thinking of himself as a pathological killer. But the fact remained that the long years of war had given him a taste of seeing men slump before him, spurting blood and gore from gaping wounds. He had discovered that he was able to kill with a sensation that often went beyond enjoyment and into the realms of exhilaration.

But he was able to justify such a feeling. He was fighting for a purpose. Nothing so abstract as justice or glory. His aim was to return home and work the farm with Jamie: and every Rebel who fell at his hand was a step closer to peace and happiness on the prairies of Iowa.

How many more steps, though? The soldiers in Hartford Gap and the defenceless actors added up to a great many corpses. But how closer was the farm with its green pasture and golden wheat fields basking under the mid-west sun? Not three stinking seconds or three lousy feet. And he'd known it while the Rebs were being torn to pieces by the explosion and the actors were spilling blood under the slashing, stabbing blades. There had been not the slightest tremor of excitement in the acts of killing. Cold, calculated self-preservation had been the sole motivation. And when there was no other factor but this, the easiest course was to get the hell out to where every rock or tree trunk, building or hill crest did not represent cover to an enemy: and to where a man could rest wherever he wanted when he was tired.

Hedges looked around at the troopers, incongruously attired

in white Stetsons, embroidered shirts, fancy pants and high boots – the Easterners' idea of what a cowpoke wore for work. If he, with something clear-cut and solid to fight for, felt like turning his back on the war, how much more bitter must be the thoughts of these men?

"Even seeing you dressed up like a dude ain't no fun, Captain," Forrest said dully, once more reading in the hooded eyes something of what was running through the mind behind them.

Like the others, he wore a hand-tooled leather gunbelt with a tied down holster. The ivory grip of a shiny revolver poked up from the ornately stitched leather. Although tired, he was still fast. In the time it took the watching troopers to blink their red-rimmed eyes, the sergeant crouched, drew and squeezed the trigger. It was all part of a single co-ordinated, fluid movement. The gun muzzle was in line with Hedges' heart when the report cracked apart the dawn silence. The Captain made no move to draw his own gun.

"Christ, Frank!" Billy Seward muttered.

Forrest showed a cold grin. Hedges matched it.

"Lousy test, sergeant," the Captain said softly.

Forrest shrugged. "You knew?"

Rhett had drawn his gun and was checking the cylinder. "Frigging toys loaded with blanks!" he announced.

"We gonna hang around here all day playing kids' games?" Hal Douglas complained.

Hedges withdrew the theatrical prop slowly and scaled it out into the river. He stooped, picked up the Colt and holstered it. Then he lifted the Spencer and tossed it up on to the driver's seat of the stage. He climbed aboard and unwound the reins from the brake lever. The troopers divided their weary attention between the Captain and the sergeant.

"You guys can do whatever the hell you like," Hedges drawled easily. "I'm gonna find me a place to sleep."

Abruptly every eye was concentrated upon him and they were no longer dull and lifeless. Instead, they expressed quizzical surprise at the indifferent attitude and uncharacteristic sentiments of the Captain.

"You sound like a man giving up," Forrest sneered.

Hedges shook his head. "Just a man who doesn't need the hired hands no more," he answered. "I don't figure to have to fight my way into Richmond. And when I get there, there'll be just Jefferson Davis and me." He showed a tired grin. "And he ain't no Frank Forrest with a gun, I hear."

The sneer became a snarl. "You ain't running out on us, Hedges!" the sergeant barked.

"I got room to take six," the Captain replied evenly, then fed ice into his eyes. "But not passengers. And not toting toy guns."

Hedges concealed his surprise at Forrest's reaction. He had expected the mean-faced sergeant to grasp the opportunity to opt out of the war, and there was no doubt that the other five troopers would have followed him. But Forrest hurled the shiny gun out into the river and snatched up his Colt and Spencer. The others followed his example, not attempting to mask their disappointment. Forrest reached up and hauled himself on to the seat beside Hedges. The others climbed into the cramped passenger section, sharing the restricted space with three large trunks.

The Captain released the brake lever and slapped the reins over the backs of the team. The wheels made sucking noises as they turned on the muddy trail.

"You got your bluff called, uh Captain?" Forrest said after a lengthy period of silence.

"No bluff," Hedges replied.

"Because you had the real guns and we only had actors' junk?"

"What do you think?"

Forrest gave a harsh laugh. "That you'd have blasted me and every man who tried to back out with me."

Hedges considered the suggestion for a few moments, then gave a curt nod. "Deserters deserve nothing less.'

"You're okay, Captain," Forrest said, raising his voice so the men inside the stage could hear. "Forget what I said back there about you being more careful than you oughta be. Takes a brave man to go gunning for a President on his own."

Hedges leaned to the side and spat. "Am I supposed to be flattered, sergeant?" he asked, eyeing the stand of timber ahead.

"Just grateful," Forrest replied. "It ain't gonna be easy, knocking off a President. You'll need help. It won't be any stand-up-in-the-street straightforward shoot out, man to man."

"You talk like a man with experience," Hedges said sardonically as he steered the team around a curve in the trail and into the wood.

Forrest shrugged. "Got me a Mexican governor down in Sonora one time, Captain," he replied conversationally. "But I had me three gunslingers along. Had to blast maybe ten or a dozen guards before we reached the governor."

Hedges angled the stage off the trail and weaved between the trees, looking for a safe place to halt and rest. "How much you get paid for that job?"

"Nothin'," Forrest answered. "This guy promised bounties on Apache scalps and didn't deliver. Me and the boys killed him 'cause he cheated us. Cut him up a little before we put bullets in him. Made a lot of noise."

"Must have been a barrel of fun," Hedges said wryly as he reined the team to a halt in a glade screened from the trail.

"It wasn't that so much," Forrest said reflectively as Hedges jumped down and started to unhitch the team. "But it was what got my rep really started. Just walking into the fancy house, blasting the guards and giving the governor a hard time. The name Frank Forrest really started to mean something."

"And now you've been away a long time," Hedges supplied.

Forrest leapt to the ground and nodded. "That's right, Captain. And people got short memories. On top of which, a lot of guys have creamed a lot of other guys in this war. When it's over they'll all be shooting off their mouths about it."

"Hey, that's right," Billy Seward exclaimed as he climbed out of the stage, the others following him. "But how many guys'll be able to say they blasted the Reb President?"

Only Seward and Forrest grinned their delight at the prospect. Weariness had reasserted an eyelid drooping grip on the others.

"Make camp," Hedges instructed and there was a sudden flurry of activity as the three tents were off-loaded and set up in the lush clearing.

One of the trunks contained food and coffee beans but the effects of the meal eaten at Hartford Gap were still with the men and sleep was the prime necessity. The surge of energy created within Forrest and Seward by the prospect of being known as the presidential killers, earned the two men the first guard duty. They griped, and Hedges accepted this as a good sign as he stretched out on a blanket in the tent he had claimed for himself. After a period of prolonged rest it was likely that the other four troopers would share the renewed enthusiasm of Forrest and Seward. It was pure luck, of course, Hedges realized as he stared up at the inner angle of the tent roof. He could claim no credit, as a man or an officer.

When he climbed aboard the stage, he had fully intended to drive off and leave the troopers if that was the way they wanted it. A few moments later, he changed his mind. He would shoot them as deserters. It was merely good fortune that Forrest spotted the unexpressed threat. And a greater good fortune that this mission was something special. For had they been going on patrol or even into battle, the men would have been poised on a knife-edge: as ready to kill their officer as they were to slaughter the enemy.

But now Forrest had supplied the final injection of luck which played into Hedges' hand. He had dangled before himself and the others a prize which, to them, was far more desirable than Hedges' simple aim of a peaceful life on the Iowa farm. As the Captain closed his eyes, he reflected that to men such as those he led, the successful end of this mission could be termed glory. Not in respect of striking a blow which might end the war. Nor even in overcoming overwhelming odds to strike the blow. Rather, in the knowledge that their fellow men would become aware of what they had done and pay homage by means of fear-based respect.

Then Hedges forced his mind to become a blank, receptive to the anxious pressure of sleep. The mechanics of how it had happened didn't matter. The men were well fed and in time they would be rested. And when that was achieved, he would once again be leading what he considered to be the best small fighting unit in the Federal Army.

"You reckon the Captain really would have gunned us down, Frank?" he heard Seward ask as the first gentle wave of sleep's tide washed out the final traces of anxiety and left his mind smooth and unruffled.

"I would have, in his position," Forrest replied gruffly.

"Hot dog!" Seward gasped.

"More like apple pie," Forrest replied.

"Uh?"

"What you get for dessert!" Forrest told the young killer.

Hedges dived into sleep with a grin curling back his lips. He was roused six hours later, by Bell and Scott at the end of their guard duty. The pale orb of the sun filtering through a thick layer of grey cloud fixed the time at close to eleven o'clock. He allowed the men to stay in their tents until it was far beyond its high point: and the time was after three when he started a small fire and the men crawled out into the mid-afternoon light, nostrils twitching to the aroma of boiling coffee.

Sleep had taken the redness from their eyelids and diffused it across their cheeks. The Captain's razor was passed around and stubble was scraped from jaws and throats. Hot coffee made stale crackers digestible.

"I feel like a new man!" Bob Rhett announced expansively after he had removed the dressing from his head and bathed the scabbed scar.

"Which one of you guy's he been having?" Forrest snapped, with mock anger and a raking look of faked suspicion.

The others grinned. Rhett scowled.

"It's gettin' so I can't open my mouth without putting a foot in it!" the New Englander complained.

"A foot?" Forrest exclaimed incredulously.

"Ah, Bob!" John Scott put in. "You let our secret out. These guys know I'm the only one with that much."

"You're sure as hell a big one!" Seward countered, giggling. "What'd you say, Captain?"

Hedges was sitting on the running board of the stage, smoking a cigarette, quietly content that the ribbing of Rhett, and any other man who left himself open, was a further sign that the troopers' morale had been given a boost. He swallowed the coffee remaining in his mug and flicked the cigarette into the heart of the dying fire.

"That they come in all shapes and sizes, trooper," he said as he stood up, and suddenly grinned to take the sting out of the taunt. "We've all gotta be pricks to be in the middle of Reb country dressed up like California dudes."

"The kind that's needed to shaft old Jefferson Davis!" Roger Bell countered.

"So let's get on the job," Hedges ordered.

With the team hitched, Hedges again took the reins and Forrest shared the box seat with him while the others climbed inside the stage. More than fourteen hours had slid into history since the last rain had fallen and the trail was firmer beneath the hooves of the team and the rims of the wheels. Hedges was able to keep the stage moving at a fast pace for most of the time as the afternoon light faded into retreat under the relentless pressure of evening gloom.

They saw no more soldiers, either out on the trail or in the many small hamlets they passed through. Civilians eyed the stage and its occupants curiously and at first this caused a degree of apprehension to cloud the minds and eyes of the troopers. But then Hedges realized the reason for the strange looks cast in their direction. The stage on its own was an oddity, with the garishly painted signs on the side. And the theatrical costumes of its driver and passengers were obviously an even more outlandish sight to the Virginian plantation workers.

After he had passed this explanation on to the men, the stage rolled sedately through the tiny communities minus its previous burden of nervous tension. Fists relaxed their grip around revolver butts and easy smiles replaced strained expressions.

The first large town they reached was called Pineville, straddling the Roanoke River. A faint orange glow in the sky – reflection of the town's lights on the low cloud – was the initial indication that the stage was heading for a much larger community than any it had past through since the troopers commandeered it. The trail cut through a rocky gorge and emerged at the top of a gentle incline. Hedges hauled on the reins and locked the brake.

"What about it, Captain?" Forrest asked as the troopers inside the stage leaned out of the windows to see what was causing the hold-up.

The trail ran down the slope in a curve, providing a wide thoroughfare through the thickly wooded terrain. The town started at the foot of the incline extending eastwards for about a mile and spreading out to north and south for perhaps half a mile at the widest point. It was completely surrounded by forest and the river cut a silvered diagonal through the buildings, northwest to south-east. It was a well-planned town with straight streets crossing each other at broad intersections. Milling and lumber industries were concentrated at the river banks on the south side. The mid-town section was brightly lit by gas. The residential areas surrounding this oasis of light had a peaceful, respectable look.

"I think we gotta go through," Hedges replied after raking his slitted eyes around the fringes of the town. Trails left town in many directions at irregular intervals but there was none which offered a by-pass route.

"Ain't Richmond, is it?" Billy Seward asked.

"Glad your shooting is better than your geography, Billy," Bob Rhett told him.

"Up yours!" the younger trooper snarled.

"Promises, promises," Rhett retorted in falsetto tones.

"Ain't no way round," Forrest agreed.

"Act natural," Hedges called to the men inside the stage as he urged the team down the incline.

"You just pretend, Bob," John Scott muttered to the New Englander.

There were few people and few lights to be seen at the edge of town. Most of the substantially built frame houses were in darkness and looked empty. The hoofbeats of the team and creaking of the ancient stage resounded against the blank facades on either side. The street became paved as it ran through the business section and there were more people on the sidewalks. All were dressed in their Sunday best and turned recently scrubbed or newly shaved faces to look towards the lumbering stage. Some consulted pocket watches. Others smiled warmly. More waved enthusiastically. All were hurrying towards the brightly lit midtown area.

"They look kinda gay," Rhett said, waving back to the citizens of Pineville like a visiting dignitary.

"It's all in your mind," Roger Bell muttered.

"And we know where Bob's mind is," Hal Douglas countered.

"That's why he talks so much crap," John Scott put in.

"Will you look at the boobs on that dame in the red dress!" Billy Seward exclaimed.

"Billy!" The name was growled by Forrest as the sergeant fixed a falsely warm smile on his mean features and nodded towards the happy crowd pressing excitedly along the sidewalks.

"Yeah, Frank?" Seward called up.

"Business before pleasure."

"Sure be a pleasure to give her the business," Seward muttered softly.

"Forget it, Billy," Douglas told him. "She's old enough to be your mother."

"She couldn't be," Rhett hissed in a vindictive tone. "I saw her ring. She's married."

Like the others, Hedges was going through the motions of responding to the greetings, but his smile and easy attitude comprised a cover for a nagging anxiety. The reason for his concern was not an easily identifiable one: such as the fact that they were seven Union soldiers moving deeper into the heart of a Confederate town. Rather, it arose from a suspicion based upon the insecure foundation of a hunch.

Then the team hauled the stage into the broad, gaslit square at the very centre of Pineville and his anxiety was seen to be well-founded.

"Jesus Christ Almighty!" Forrest rasped. "Now what do we do?"

The Pineville Playhouse was on the north side of the square, a two storey frame building spilling a lot of light from its crowded foyer. Multi-coloured gas mantles hissed around the marquee, illuminating the lettering on a square of canvas:

For One Night Only
THE JOHN FORD TOURING COMPANY
in
The West As It Really Is

"Don't reckon he's gonna help us," Hedges muttered in reply as he angled the stage across the square to where a small man in a tuxedo was beckoning frantically.

"What the hell we gonna do to help ourselves then?" Forrest growled.

"Play along," Hedges replied with a grin, jerking free of his anxiety now he knew the true situation: leaving his mind free to deal with it. "Evenin'," he called down to the man in the tux, whose agitation could be seen in the sweat on his crimson face and the constant blinking of his watery eyes.

"Mr. Ford?" His voice was squeaky, as if he had just completed a long, loud speech.

"Appearing in person," Hedges boomed dramatically.

"You're late," the man accused, then brandished his hand as if to wave aside potential excuses. "Never mind. You're here now. I'm Griffiths. Theatre manager. Stage door's along the side alley. You can take the rig down. You've got a little time to get ready. There's another attraction on ahead of you."

He didn't punctuate his speech, taking a deep breath before he started and running out all the words in a single sentence.

"Not animals or children, I hope?" Hedges demanded. "They're hard to follow."

Griffiths mopped his face with a large coloured handkerchief. It left his features dry and set in a mournful expression. "A hanging."

"Swinging opening," Hedges muttered as he clucked the team forward and jerked on the reins to steer them into the alley alongside the playhouse.

"What the hell's goin' to happen after that?" Forrest growled.

"The show must go on," Hedges replied as he hauled the team to a halt outside the stage door of the theatre. "Just hope the dancer's the only guy to die the death."

EDGE rode the gelding hard, galloping north in the wake of the stage. The night became colder as it grew older. But it was miles rather than time which caused the temperature drop. For once clear of the plateau the trail began to climb, meandering and sometimes making hairpin turns to gain altitude up the solid rock of the mountains.

The terrain was in the half-breed's favour. For the sharp turns in narrow gorges and the narrowness of the ledges with sheer drops on one side would force the stage driver to slow his speed. Such a trail was much easier for a lone rider to negotiate.

He ran into difficulty only once, when the trail seemed to fork, offering alternative routes to twin passes in a high ridge, black, jagged and foreboding in the silvered moonlight. The rocky surface of the trails showed no hoofmarks or wheel ruts. But the time he spent exploring several hundred yards along the trails was not wasted. It gave the gelding a respite and when Edge's narrowed eyes spotted the fresh cigar butt his mount was breathing easily again and the white foam of sweat had dried and ceased to steam from the animal's flanks.

The stogy was out, but still retained a faint trace of warmth. Edge remounted and thudded in his heels to drive the horse into a gallop. The trail continued to be as tortuous as before in reaching up to the western pass and he followed it with a calculated recklessness. He spotted the stage as he halted the gelding in the break in the ridge. As was his way, not even a mere flicker of satisfaction showed in the ice-cold blueness of his slitted eyes when he saw the rig, lurching slowly across the rocky bed of a wide but shallow stream some two hundred feet below him. Such was the clarity of the mountain air, he could hear every snarling curse uttered by the ill-tempered driver as the whip lashed across the quivering backs of the struggling team.

The angry words, the hiss of water over the rocks and the splashing and snorting of the team covered the sounds of Edge's approach. At the bank of the stream, he veered the gelding to one side and forded the ice-cold water fifty yards upstream from the trail. He stayed in the cover of a deeply shadowed rock wall until the stage was dragged clear of the water course. Apart from the driver, there was also a guard riding on the high box seat. A considerable amount of baggage was lashed to the roof behind them. The blinds had been drawn across the windows.

"You reckon you ought to rest the horses, Troy?" the elderly guard suggested.

The much younger driver had, in fact, halted the team clear of the water, but only so that he could take a tailor-made cigarette from his shirt pocket and light it. He laughed. "You ain't got no bride of a week to get home to, Bill," he answered.

The guard's laughter had a cackling tone. "Absence makes the heart grow fonder, boy," he said.

"Ain't my heart that's growing, Bill," the driver responded, picking up the whip. "If I don't get home I'm gonna bust my breeches."

"Troy, wait!" Edge said evenly, urging his horse out from behind the rock and levelling the Winchester.

"A stick up!" the guard gasped, reaching for the rifle resting on the roof behind him.

"You tired of living, old man?" Edge asked, moving the gelding in closer.

The guard halted his move, then swung around to face the half-breed again. "We ain't got no bank shipment aboard, mister," he said. "Ain't got nothin' aboard worth anyone getting shot."

Troy nodded in agreement. His face was very pale in the moonlight. The cigarette slanted from the corner of his mouth and smoke curled into his right eye. He was paralysed with fear, unable to touch the cigarette or rub his eye.

"Toss your guns down here," Edge instructed. "Hold them by the barrels."

The rifle clattered to the ground first. Then Bill's Colt. He had to hook the Remington revolver from Troy's holster and toss it down.

"Now the both of you," Edge urged. "And roust out the passengers."

The old guard climbed down carefully, his ancient bones creaking. Fear made the driver's actions even slower and stiffer.

"What you gonna do, mister?" Bill asked nervously.

"Put a bullet in you," the half-breed replied softly. The old man gasped and flattened himself against a wheel. Edge added: 'If you don't get the passengers outta that stage real quick."

The guard licked his thin lips and reached out a trembling and to turn the door handle. As the door folded back, five white faces stared out at the impassive man astride the gelding. Three of the passengers were men and two were women. Both the women were in their sixties and grey-haired.

"Please get out, folks," the guard pleaded. "If you don't, I'm the one's gonna suffer."

Edge shook his head. "You won't suffer, feller. It'll be quick." His eyes raked over the ashen-faced passengers. "And you'll have company on that long stage trail in the sky."

The passengers were galvanized into action, fighting each other in their haste to get through the narrow doorway. They gathered in a tight-knit group, careful not to get between Edge and the driver and guard. The half-breed ducked his head momentarily to peer inside the stage. It was empty.

"All I got is three dollars, mister," one of the male passengers said with a quiver in his voice.

"Save it to buy the drinks you're gonna need," Edge told him, and fixed his glinting stare on the guard. "Where'd the girl get off?" he asked.

The old man had to swallow the lump in his throat before he could speak. "Trail Forks. Back over the other side of the pass. That all you stuck us up for, mister? I'd have told you."

"That's all?" one of the women asked, irritated. "You don't want anything else from us?"

"Not me, ma'am," Edge replied, sliding the Winchester into the boot and flicking a finger against his hat-brim. "You folks got nothing I want."

His right hand was draped loosely over the butt of his holstered Colt, warning them against trying for the guns on the ground or any the passengers might be carrying.

"Well, really, frightening us all like that for such a small thing!" the irate lady complained.

Edge sighed. "If it'll make you any happier, lady, I'll shoot you," he offered softly.

The woman gave a choked cry of alarm and hurriedly, ungracefully, climbed back aboard the stage. The other passengers followed her, but more carefully, pointedly avoiding the unblinking eyes of the half-breed. They sat very erect in their seats, like wax dummies.

"On your way, fellers," Edge urged.

The driver was still rigid with fear. His movements had a mechanical quality as he climbed up on to the seat.

"What about our guns?" the guard asked, his tongue darting out to moisten his lips.

Edge spat. "You're welcome to try picking them up," he invited.

The driver yelled as the cigarette burned down to its end and seared his lips. The guard dropped his gaze from Edge's face to the hand draped over the gun butt.

"Guess the company'll have to buy us some new irons," the old man muttered, and hauled his arthritic body up on to the seat. "All right, Troy, head for home and that new wife of yours."

The driver eased the team into a slow start. The fact that they were rolling again gave the shaken passengers courage enough to look out of the window at the tall half-breed resting casually in the saddle.

Edge curled back his thin lips to show a smile. The humour did not extend to his eyes. "Sorry to have held you up," he called.

CHAPTER SEVEN

The shavetail lieutenant with the battered and badly cut face tried not to tremble as he stood in the centre of the stage, his hands tied behind his back and a noose looped around his neck. In front of him, the auditorium of the Pineville Playhouse was packed to capacity. Every seat was taken, the aisles were jammed with people sitting cross-legged and the standing area at the rear was filled to discomfort.

The gallows had been so erected that the condemned man stood on a trapdoor close to the front of the stage with its row of hissing, gas-fueled footlights. A Confederate infantry corporal stood at each side of the stage, aiming a rifle at the helpless prisoner. One of the captains commanding the unit responsible for capturing the Union officer moved on to the stage from the right wing. He flushed and gave a stiff bow as the audience greeted him with a burst of enthusiastic applause.

He waited nervously for the noise to diminish, then cleared his throat. "Ladies and gentlemen of Pineville," he announced. "As you are all aware, this Yankee intelligence agent was captured yesterday on the soil of Confederate Virginia."

There was a cheer, which he silenced with a wave of his hand. "He is the lone survivor of an enemy force which cowardly slaughtered a score of our brave soldiers. The fact that he alone escaped death is proof of how bravely our boys fought in the name of the Cause."

In the large communal dressing room below stage, Hedges and the six troopers listened with varying degrees of anxiety to what was happening above their heads.

"Ain't that what's called propaganda?" Hal Douglas muttered.

"Proper horseshit is what I call it," Forrest growled.

99

"This officer," the Rebel Captain went on, stressing the commission in the manner of an insult, "has further compounded his cowardice by ratting on his comrades." He laughed shortly. "As you can see, ladies and gentlemen, he was so frightened while we were questioning him, he kept going weak at the knees and falling on his face."

The audience exploded into laughter.

The Union men had guessed who was to be executed when, on their way to the dressing room, they passed a doorway guarded by the two corporals. The Captain had emerged from the guarded room and was recognized, confirming the guess. Fortunately, the troopers in their decorative western garb were able to hurry through into the dressing room before the Confederate officer had time to spot them as fakes.

"Now he has served his purpose," the man on stage went on after the laughter had died down. "He has told us every detail of the vile plot he and his fellow Federal spies have hatched. I will not bore you with the details. But you may rest assured that the Army of the Confederacy has taken steps to combat the plot."

He paused for an expected cheer. It came. But it was late and lacking in vigour. The majority of the audience had heard enough words and were impatient for the gruesome climax of the added attraction.

Hedges had not even considered the chance of rescuing the Lieutenant. The shavetail had failed twice – first in allowing himself to be captured, then in shooting off his mouth under torture. But there was no vindictiveness in Hedges' decision. It was based on the simple fact that the death of Jefferson Davis was more important than the life of a no-account Union Lieutenant.

"It has been decided to execute this man in public for two reasons," the Rebel Captain continued. "Firstly to show you people how we deal with enemies of the Confederacy. And secondly as a warning to any among you who may be, or may be considering, aiding the Yankee invaders."

His voice was appropriately stern as he spoke the threat. Feet shuffled uncomfortably and several throats were cleared.

In ignoring the plight of the condemned man, Hedges was able to apply his mind fully to the problem of maintaining the subterfuge of the stolen identities. And there was only one answer – to go through with the performance expected of them. To run out would surely start a hue and cry and the civilian citizenry of Pineville would not be the only ones in pursuit of the escapers. For the agitated Griffiths had revealed that the detachment of battle-weary Rebel soldiers were resting up in the town, except for two men sent on horseback to Richmond with a despatch concerning the plot against Jefferson Davis.

"This officer maintains that if he is to die, it should be by means of the firing squad," the Captain told his silent audience. "If he were an ordinary soldier as his uniform suggests, he would be accorded that honour. But beneath the uniform lurks a dirty spy. Therefore, a military tribunal consisting of myself and two fellow officers have sentenced him to hang."

The silence seemed to solidify in the tense atmosphere of the playhouse. The Captain's boot soles rasped against the boards of the stage as he turned.

"Do you have anything to say before the sentence is carried out?"

There was a large variety of costumes in the actors' trunks, but no scripts. The only indication of the subject matter treated by the troupe was evidenced by a number of cardboard signs, garishly lettered: CALIFORNIA GOLD RUSH, THE BANK RAID, GUNFIGHT SHOWDOWN, CATTLE RUSTLERS and PRAIRIE CAMPFIRE.

With the Rebel Captain close at hand and the possibility that there were other soldiers in the audience who might recognize the troopers as frauds, the choice was an obvious one. But it had an inbuilt complication, and the method Hedges used to get around this was not popular with Seward, Bell and Rhett.

"Well?" the Captain barked, leaning forward so that his face was only inches from the ravaged features of the helpless Lieutenant. "No last words?"

The Lieutenant dragged his shoulders erect and held his head high as he stared directly ahead from out of the puffed flesh around his eyes.

"Maybe his necktie's too tight!" a man shouted harshly from the audience, and drew guffaws.

"Corporal!" the Captain snapped.

The guard on the right sprang into an about-face and ducked out of sight behind the proscenium arch. He rested his rifle and gripped the lever which operated the spring-loaded trap door upon which the condemned man stood. "Ready, sir!" he reported into the tense silence gripping the playhouse.

"May God have mercy on your soul!" the Rebel Captain said to the Lieutenant, and gave a curt nod in the direction of the corporal.

The non-com snapped his eyes tight closed and wrenched down on the lever. The trap opened beneath the feet of the condemned man. He opened his mouth to say something but it was too late. His weight snapped the rope taut. His final breath shot his tongue forward and his teeth crunched together as his neck broke. The tip of his tongue was bitten off and spattered on to the toe of his muddy right boot. Oozing blood adhered the pulpy flesh to its resting place as the body and limbs of the dead man swung. A massed gasp rose from the audience as a single sound. Only the expressions on the faces of the watchers revealed whether the individual utterances were of shock, horror or exhileration.

"So perish all enemies of the Confederacy!" the Rebel Captain shouted dramatically. "Let the entertainment continue."

"That's us!" Hedges rasped, snatching up the sign lettered with the legend THE BANK RAID.

This was confirmed by a rap of knuckles on the door of the large under-stage room. "Five minutes, Mr. Ford," Griffiths announced anxiously. "Will you be ready?"

"Yeah!" the Union Captain replied, then lowered his voice. "As we'll ever be."

Applause broke out from the audience as Griffiths ran up the steps and elbowed the non-com executioner out of the way, reaching for the ropes to draw the curtains across the stage.

"Clear the stage, please!" he instructed the Captain, doing his best not to look at the battered face atop the still swaying body of the dead Lieutenant. "We must get on."

He waited a few moments, until the Captain had beckoned to the two corporals and the three soldiers were moving towards the gallows: then he stepped between the curtains and held up his hands to silence the final handclaps.

"And now, ladies and gentlemen," he announced. "On to the main part of the programme. Mr. John Ford, the distinguished actor and his band of players will present a series of playlets depicting life in the Far West of this great country of ours. The Pineville Playhouse is indeed honoured to welcome this famous acting troupe and it is with the utmost certainty that I can promise you an evening of fine entertainment. The plays will commence just as soon as the items used in the first section of the programme have been removed from the stage. Thank you."

"They gotta be good to keep me interested after what I just seen!" a man shouted.

"Damn right!" another man agreed.

"They will be," Griffiths responded, a trifle nervously, and ducked back behind the curtains before his lack of conviction became too obvious.

The body had been removed and the two corporals were in the act of carrying off the gallows under the direction of the Captain. Griffiths worked the lever which raised the trapdoor back into place. The officer gave a curt nod of farewell and went into the shadows to the left of the stage. The agitated playhouse manager looked across the empty boards, running a crooked finger around the inside of his dress shirt collar and mopping the beads of sweat from his forehead.

"Christ!" he muttered. "Scenery and props!"

A mumble of conversation sounded from the auditorium. It seemed to Griffiths to contain a heavy note of impatience.

"We don't use 'em," Bob Rhett said.

Griffiths was startled by the voice, then gave a gasp of amazement as he turned and saw the speaker – and Seward and Bell coming up the steps behind the New Englander.

"Just these crazy outfits!" Seward rasped gruffy, and thrust the cardboard sign into the hands of the blinking Griffiths. "Stick this out and let's get on with it."

A wooden stand was leaning against the wall and as the stamping of feet augmented the oral discontent of the waiting audience, Griffiths hurriedly unfolded it, rested the sign on the brackets and thrust the announcement through the side gap in the curtains. A cheer rose. And a few seconds later, as Griffiths reacted to a pointing finger from Rhett and hauled on the rope, the swishing open of the curtains signalled a sudden, expectant silence.

Rhett stood down-stage centre, attired in a black gown buttoned high to the throat and sweeping down to brush against the boards at the hem. Heavy padding beneath the bodice provided a good imitation of a feminine figure. His own slim shape needed no artificial aids to complete the picture. Rouge, lipstick and thick eye make-up caused the handsome face to match the body and the final touch was a shoulder-length blonde wig.

A number of the more outgoing men in the audience were sufficiently fooled to greet the New Englander with admiring whistles. And it was Rhett alone who captured their fancy, even though Bell and Seward were also attired as women. For they were obvious fakes, despite the fine meshed veils which hung from beneath broad brimmed hats to drape their unpainted features. Their postures were wrong, lacking the natural grace of Rhett and despite the padding beneath their white dresses they looked in no way feminine.

"Ladies and gentlemen," Rhett opened, pitching his voice to a higher falsetto than normal. "We crave your indulgence in the matter of scenery and ask you to enter into the spirit of what may be termed a new method of acting – a method in which you, the audience, play parts as important as we the actors. For you must use your imaginations to paint the settings in which we act out the drama. I will tell you only that this stage is a bank in a town of the south west. I am the teller and my colleagues are customers. The actions will speak for themselves."

"Don't he go on," Hal Douglas whispered.

"He's goddamn enjoying it," Forrest muttered, surprised. "After all that griping at wearing a dress and painting his face up."

"If he don't hurry it up, Billy's goin' to belt him," Scott warned. "I can see it happenin'."

"If he don't hurry it up, I'll cut him in a place that'll make him more like a woman than any dress or paint," Hedges breathed.

The four men stood just off-stage left, their low voices muffled by bandanas formed into masks across the lower halves of their faces and tied at the back. They were dressed in western style, but their costumes were less ornate than those they had been wearing previously. Each carried a Spencer rifle and had Colts in tied down holsters on their right thighs. Across the stage they could see where Griffiths stood in sweating awe, listening to Rhett hamming up his speech, explaining how a play without scenery allowed each member of the audience to witness the drama in an individual way.

"I reckon it's 'cause you can't afford to buy none!" a man called wryly.

"But enough of this," Rhett concluded, ignoring the comment as he bowed elegantly from the waist. "The play's the thing."

"Wondered if you'd ever get around to it," another heckler yelled.

Rhett flashed a bright smile and backed away from the hissing footlights, then turned to face Seward and Bell across a space of three feet. Now that they were as much the centre of attention as the New Englander, the two became woodenly rigid with stage-fright.

There had been no kind of rehearsal below stage and as the moment of going on stage approached, Hedges had considered calling a halt to the crazy charade and trying to lead the men out of the playhouse unobserved and ordering them to shoot anybody who stood in their way. He had no doubt the troopers would fall in with such a plan, choosing to take their chances against the detachment of Rebel soldiers rather than face the civilian audience. But the ultimate aim of the mission had to be considered – and if they could maintain the disguise of actors they would have a better chance of reaching Richmond and the Confederate president than if they were spotted as Union infiltrators. Rhett's sudden announcement that he had acted in school plays had heavily influenced the Captain's decision and Hedges had willingly allowed the New Englander to assume responsibility for what was to occur on the playhouse stage.

"Good morning, Mrs. Seward," Rhett opened. "How's Mr. Seward?"

Seward remained resolutely silent and Rhett leaned towards him.

"I beg your pardon? I didn't catch that?"

"He's okay," Seward responded tightly, deeply.

"My, you have a bad throat," Rhett adlibbed expertly. "Do you wish to make a deposit or a withdrawal today?"

"I wanna take some cash out," Seward replied in the same deep tone.

Bell shuffled his feet.

"And how's Miss Bell this fine morning?" Rhett asked with a broad smile, leaning to the side to look around Seward.

"Just great," Bell growled.

"Christ, there's an epedemic of the sore throat out west," a heckler yelled in delight.

A ripple of laughter ran through the audience. Rhett turned his head slightly and glared venomously at Seward and Bell. When his profile came into the view of the audience again, his face was wreathed in a bright smile.

"How much, Mrs. Seward?"

"How much what?"

Rhett sighed and stamped his foot. "How much do you wish to withdraw?"

"Oh, yeah. Hundred bucks. And hurry it up so I can get off the . . . outa the damn bank."

"Yeah, hurry it up and get him off, sweetie," another heckler yelled. "He stinks."

Seward whirled, and stared into a wall of blackness above the glowing mantles of the footlights. Behind the masking veil, his features were changed from a scowl of anger into a frown of confusion.

"Billy!" Bell warned in a rasping whisper.

The men off-stage were supposed to wait for a signal from

Rhett before making an entrance, but Hedges saw the sign of Seward's flaring temper and stepped out on to the stage, bringing up the Spencer. The other three hesitated only a moment before crowding along behind him, levelling their rifles.

"Everybody freeze!" the Captain ordered, too loudly.

"Yeah, this is a stick up!" Forrest supplement.

"Foul up, more like," a man in the audience countered, and drew several grunts of agreement.

On the far side of the stage, out of public sight, the playhouse manager worked frantically at mopping sweat from his face. His free hand hovered nervously above the rope which operated the curtains.

"Oh, my goodness!" Rhett exclaimed, thrusting his arms high above his head. "This is terrible."

"And how, lady!" From the audience.

"Get 'em up!" Scott snarled, waving his gun between Bell and Seward.

As both men raised their hands, Bell's padded breasts slipped down inside his dress to form a bulge at his stomach. A roar of laughter burst from the audience.

"He said up!" a voice cut through the noise.

"You can have every dollar in the bank, so long as you don't harm us!" Rhett stormed on, struggling to be heard above the laughter as Bell attempted to reshape his figure.

"Shoot 'em and end our agony!" somebody cat-called as Bell succeeded in getting one piece of padding back into place.

"Please don't shoot!" Rhett pleaded, dropping to his knees and clasping his hands together in an attitude of prayer. His painted face was twisted into an expression of anguish.

"Just hand over the money!" Forrest snarled, stepping up close to Rhett and shoving the muzzle of the Spencer hard against his chest. The barrel sank deep into the padding.

"Hey, that ain't even a dame!" a voice complained. "I bin gettin' the hots for a guy."

"What we gonna do?" Forrest roared through the din which was now part laughter, part angry hissing.

A subtle difference in the sergeant's tone told Hedges that

this was not a spontaneous line in the impromptu play. He leaned close to Forrest to be heard above the uproar.

"Let's give 'em a big finish," he snarled.

The familiar mean grin lit cold fires in Forrest's eyes "You mean—"

"Act naturally," Hedges confirmed. "Lights out first."

The officer and the non-com whirled together, drawing their Colts. For as long as it took them to fire three shots each, the greater part of the audience remained unaware of the fact that the shooting was not a part of the play. The troopers on stage had the advantage of knowing that the guns were the genuine articles, loaded with live ammunition. As the last of the footlight gas mantles was shattered, plunging the stage into darkness, every person in the theatre realized the truth of what was happening. The hissing was suddenly ominously louder as the unburned gas escaped through the fractured pipes, permeating the air with its nauseous miasma.

Women began to scream and men to shout. People rose from their seats and fought frantically to reach the doors, blocked solid by those who had been standing at the back or squatting in the aisles. The house lights on the walls at both sides were turned low, but emitted a glow sufficient for the men on the stage to see the massed panic.

"What's happening?" Griffiths screamed, rushing out on to the stage.

"They're running out on us!" Forrest yelled "But they ain't asking for their money back."

He emptied the Colt into the struggling mass of humanity, then thrust the gun back in the holster and levelled the Spencer from his hip A woman and two men went down with screams, pouring blood from gaping wounds. Trampling feet stomped them into silence and erupted fresh blood from burst skin. Hedges, Scott and Douglas fired their handguns into the midst of the struggling throng as Seward and Bell tore off their dresses to reveal that they were attired just like the others underneath. Both wore gunbelts and drew Colts to add to the wanton, murderous fire.

"What are you doing?" Griffiths screamed.

"Shooting us a few Southerners," Seward answered casually, turning towards the playhouse manager. Both men began to cough. "Real gas, ain't it?"

He shot the man in the tuxedo, firing into the belly Griffiths coughed again and a great spray of blood erupted from his open mouth as he doubled up and fell forward.

There were two doors at the rear of the auditorium and both of them were open now, as the Union troopers continued to pour rifle and revolver fire into the panicked audience. Following the lead of Hedges, the men aimed at the struggling forms in the doorways, partially blocking the escape routes with dead and wounded. There was no return of fire, either because nobody had come to the theatre carrying a gun, or because everybody considered retreat more urgent than retaliation.

"Enough!" Hedges yelled. "Let's get out of here."

"And leave these fish in the barrel?" Forrest shouted between wracking coughs. The bandana mask had slipped and his lips were curled back to match the cold grin of his eyes. He pumped more shots towards the rear of the auditorium and saw men and women crumple.

"They been battered enough," Hedges yelled at him, and coughed violently "Pretty soon they're gonna fry."

"Jesus, he's right!" Rhett screamed, turning and leaping across the slumped form of Griffiths.

Coughing and retching, the others went in the wake of the New Englander. But whereas he started down the steps towards the dressing room, Douglas led the rest towards the stage door.

"Where the hell are you going?" Hedges called down the steps.

"I'm not walking around in public dressed like this!" Rhett shrieked in reply, jerking up the hem of the gown to show he had adopted the role of a woman right down to his skin.

"You look like an angel," Hedges told him sardonically. "And you could just be one if you don't get your ass up here and out of this building pretty damn quick."

Rhett hesitated only a moment, then scrambled back up the steps and ran in pursuit of Hedges, hoisting the hem of his gown up to his bare knees.

Outside in the alley, the other troopers waited in a group behind the cover of the stage coach, long ago unhitched from the team. All were looking down towards the lighted square, where the first escapers from the playhouse were streaming into freedom. Many of the women were still raising anguished screams. Hedges realized that even if nobody thought to send a message to the army, the soldiers would soon be doubling towards the playhouse, seeking the reason for the noise.

"Let's go get us some horses," Hedges instructed.

"We'll make sure to get a nice gentle animal for the lady," Seward giggled.

"I can see I'm never goin' to be able to live this down," Rhett gasped as he ran with the others towards the end of the alley furtherest from the square.

"Just concentrate on plain living, Bob," Scott urged as they emerged on to a quiet, unlit street.

Following the Captain, they turned east and were soon able to run faster than at the start, as they breathed the final fumes of gas out of their lungs. As they put distance between themselves and the playhouse the extraneous sounds diminished and the thud of their running footsteps was bounced loudly between the facades of the flanking buildings.

They found a livery stable at the extreme eastern end of Pineville. The owner, like most other citizens of the town, had gone out for an evening at the theatre. With other survivors of the shooting and trampling, he stood in the square outside the building, watching as the grey-uniformed soldiers threw a cordon around the playhouse. The panic was over now and while some women wept out their shock most of the crowd just gaped on in stunned silence as they thought about the many still forms left inside.

"I can smell gas!" a sergeant yelled.

"They shot out the lights," a civilian responded.

"Christ Almighty, why didn't somebody tell us?" the Captain responsible for the execution exclaimed. "Everybody back. Back up there!"

Only the side door through which the Union troopers escaped

was open. Those in the foyer had been allowed to swing closed after the final member of the audience had run clear. The gas rushing out through the shattered gas mantles of the footlights built up in menacing layers of danger across the auditorium. The soldiers began to withdraw from their positions and urged the rubbernecks further across the square.

"Where's the main cut-off valve?" the Captain demanded.

There was no answer. The build-up of gas expanded still further and was ignited simultaneously by ten low burning mantles around the auditorium walls. The explosion was awesome in sight, sound and effect. The roof of the playhouse was rocketed high into the air as all four walls were hurled outwards. Flaming debris – timber, seats, scenery and carpets – streaked into the hot, brilliantly lit night air. The blast lifted people bodily and slammed them down. Flying timber and glass smashed into vulnerable flesh. Ears rang agonizingly with the sharp report then roared with its aftermath so that those at the rear of the crowd could not hear the terrified screams of those at the front.

The man who owned the livery had been at the front. A scaling pane of glass severed his head from his neck. A piece of flaming carpet wrapped itself around his falling body and set light to his clothes. His gouting blood put out the flames. More than a score of others died just as horribly. Three times this number – soldiers and civilians – suffered mutilation or burning and lived to cry aloud their agony. In the roaring flames of the burning building the square was black with charring and crimson with bleeding. The screams of the injured pierced the crackling of flames to reach the east-bound trail along which the troopers steered their stolen mounts.

"Seems like our play bombed," Bob Rhett said with a giggle as the men looked back to where a thick column of black smoke reached into the sky, reflecting the orange, blue and red of the flames which created it.

"Had to," Forrest responded, spitting. "Putting it on after a hangin'."

"We did all right," Hedges told the men, as he heeled his

horse into a gallop. "We had lousy parts, but the execution was terrific."

They raced forward to Richmond.

EDGE back-tracked to where the trails forked and followed the one that wound up towards the eastern pass. From the ridge, he had a panoramic view across a broad valley, green and peaceful looking in the pale moonlight. Built on the northern slope was a large, two-storey ranch-house with wide windows from which the owner could look out and survey his extensive domain. This was comprised of several hundred acres of grazing upon which better than five thousand head of cattle roamed at will. The spread was ten times bigger than any of those surrounding Jerusalem.

There was just one lighted window in the house and Edge used this as a beacon to home in, going down a hard-packed trail that curved towards the impressive ranch. It opened out into a broad area between the house and several outbuildings then narrowed again on the far side to swoop down into the valley before rising towards an eastern pass broad enough to give passage to a cattle drive.

The buildings were long-established, but well cared for, recently painted in black and white. Window glass had a high gloss in the moonlight. A buckboard was parked in front of the stoop, with a horse harnessed between the shafts. The animal's coat had a healthy sheen in the wedge of light from the window. It and the rig were in the same fine condition as the house and the spread surrounding it.

Had anybody been watching, even idly, the trail down from the pass, they would have surely seen Edge's approach. Aware of this, the half-breed had made no attempt at stealth, riding tall in the saddle at an easy jog-trot. But once in the cover of the storage barns and stables without drawing either a call of welcome or a shouted challenge, he altered his tactics.

He dismounted and tied the gelding to the low branch of a shade tree in front of a water-barrel outside a stable. Then he slid the Winchester from the boot and moved to a corner from where his hooded eyes could survey the front of the house. There was still just the one window with a light behind it. The drape curtains were drawn back but a heavy netting partially masked the room's interior, reducing shapes to fuzzy outlines. But Edge had a clear enough view across the intervening space and through the window to determine three people in the room – two men and a woman. One of the men and the woman remained stationary against an orange glow from the fireplace. The second man was constantly moving – pacing and whirling, often gesticulating with his arms and head. The sturdy walls of the house trapped all sounds within it, but Edge guessed that a one-sided argument was in progress.

The half-breed could be a man of patience when the occasion demanded it and this was just such an occasion. The fact that the buckboard was parked outside with the horse still hitched suggested that somebody would leave soon. He could only wonder whether the departing person would be carrying the bag with the money. It would be best if that happened, because the spreaad was a big one and the house large enough to hold a great many hands.

So Edge waited, the rifle cold in his hands: prepared to enter the house and take his chances against as many guns as were in there, but hopeful it would not be necessary. The odds were against it, he figured, since any man who owned such a rich spread would be unlikely to need stolen money to pay his bills.

The wait lasted less than fifteen minutes. The man who was angry strode out of sight and the couple followed him. A few seconds later, a rectangle of light showed at the transom above the solid front door. Then the door swung open and a voice spilled out into the night – loud and angry.

"So take her! And I never want to see her again. Don't invite me to the wedding and if you breed any kids, be sure they know they don't have a grandfather."

The speaker moved into the light – a big, broad-shouldered man with iron grey hair clipped short and a deeply-lined, heavily tanned face from which his green eyes shone with an angry light. His daughter – the blonde Edge had spanked and, presumably, the one who had ridden the stage with the money – had drawn a lot of her good looks from him. She was urged out across her father's body and on to the stoop by the beefy young prize-fighter who had taken a dive in Jerusalem – David Jefferson. It was Jefferson who carried the bag with the money in it.

He wore a pained expression of injured innocence as he halted and half-turned to address the man who was more than twice his age. "We made a bargain, sir," he reminded. "As soon as I had the money to give Julia all she's enjoyed in the past, we'd have your blessing. Won't you just come out and look?"

"Give my blessing to a thief?" the grey-haired man retorted.

"There was no other way, Mr. Gold," Jefferson pleaded as the girl tried to pull him towards the buckboard. "And it wasn't stealing, not really. Gambling's a sin. You've always said it."

"So's stealing, only worse," the old man snarled. "You cheated to get what you wanted." His blazing eyes swung from Jefferson to his daughter and back again. "Both of you. And you got others to cheat with you. Even Howard, by God. So I've got no bad conscience about reneging on my promise. You got each other, which is what you wanted. All you're missing is my blessing. Now get out of this valley and don't ever come back into it."

He stepped back into the hallway, grasped the edge of the door and slammed it viciously closed. The light behind the transom went out. And moment's later, as Jefferson helped the girl up on to the buckboard, the large window of the sitting room faded. Just the orange flickering of a fire showed through the lace netting. Against it, Jefferson and the girl were silhouettes. She had her head bowed and Edge heard the sounds of quiet sobbing just before her husband-to-be put one arm around her shoulders and used his other hand to flick the reins across the back of the horse. The buckboard jerked forward and started along the trail towards the wide way out of the valley.

"Turn around slow," a man whispered, soft but harsh.

If there had been just the one, Edge might have started slow and then whirled. But once his attention was drawn away from the departing buckboard and he became aware that he was not alone among the out-buildings, he heard the sounds of two men breathing. The first man he saw was the emaciated stake-holder. He was levelling a Colt at the half-breed. Howy McNally, who

114

was really Howard Gold and looked as much like his sister as she did her father, stood six feet to the right. He held an old-fashioned Colt revolving rifle.

The door of the barn behind them was open. Both were red eyed from sleeping and pieces of the straw in which they had been resting clung to their clothes.

"Rest the rifle against the wall, mister," the youngster with the battered face instructed. "Slow, like you turned. And don't try nothing stupid. We don't want nobody to get hurt."

"I've already been hurt," Edge replied easily, setting down the Winchester. "Real bad – in the bankroll."

The thin man looked just as scared holding the gun as he had back in Jerusalem when he had been holding the money. "We should explain," he said.

"The explanation I can work out for myself," Edge replied. "What you should do is pay me what I'm owed."

"Or you'll do what?" the younger man sneered.

Edge curled back his lips in a grin that failed to reach his cold eyes. "Maybe take advantage of the fact that you don't want to hurt anybody," he said.

He drew. His upper arm did not move a fraction. But from his elbow to his fingertips the speed of the draw was a blur. At one split-second the Colt nestled harmlessly in his holster. In the next it was in his fist and pointing between the eyes of Howard Gold. It was a calculated risk, but of a kind upon which his survival had depended so many times. Gold might have fired in a reflex action and the thin man might have squeezed his trigger from simple shock.

For long seconds, the far off lowing of many head of beef was all that broke the silence trapped in the valley.

"If you guys don't lower the irons somebody's sure gonna get hurt," the half-breed said softly.

"You can't blast both of us before one of us gets you," Gold rasped, licking his lips.

"Chance I'm willing to take," Edge replied in the same easy tone. "You know I'm a gambling man."

The thin man's Colt clattered to the ground. He cleared his

throat to get rid of the lump of fear. "Don't spoil it, Howy," he pleaded. "Not now it's all over. Nobody's got hurt yet."

The tongue did some more moistening as the puffed eyes became clouded with thought. Then he lowered the ancient rifle and rested it against the wall. "What now?" he asked sullenly.

"We'll go and collect my winnings," Edge told him, waving the Colt to beckon the thin man across to stand next to Gold.

"Fat chance you've got," Gold sneered.

"I reckon it's in the bag," Edge replied.

CHAPTER EIGHT

The troopers veered away from trails and turnpikes as they crossed eastern Virginia. They rode at night and rested during the days. They stole only once – clothing for Bob Rhett so that he could dispense with the gown and garish make-up. For the rest, they bought what they wanted – one man entering a town and going to the store while the others remained hiding outside. They spared the horses as much as possible to avoid the need of obtaining fresh mounts.

All could see the wisdom of Hedges' plan for they often spotted Rebel patrols and knew from rumours picked up in towns on shopping expeditions that the soldiers were seeking them. By staying out of sight and committing no crimes they gave the enemy no opportunity to pin-point their position and concentrate the search.

They saw a marker pointing the way to Richmond in the grey light of breaking dawn on the fifth day. It indicated a distance of six miles, which was too far since it would mean the troopers would cross the James River and enter the city in full daylight. And Hedges had no idea how easy it would be to find a safe place to hole up and wait until dark. Out in the country there were hiding places in plenty and the Captain led the weary-eyed and heavy-limbed troopers northwards through an area of heavily-wooded, rolling hills. He found a disused spur of the Richmond and Danville Railroad which dead-ended in a rotting locomotive shed and here the men and animals could rest. But despite the utter lack of any sign that the shed had been visited in many years, each man stood a stint of guard duty.

And there was no griping about the Captain's over-cautiousness. This did not surprise Hedges, for the attitude of the troopers had changed since shortly after their explosive departure from Pineville. It was as if the roar of igniting gas had driven home to them the seriousness of their position. The last time they had been behind enemy lines was in far off Georgia and they had been making a run for home. But now they were close to the well-protected heart of the Confederacy — and heading towards it. And as they neared their objective, their mood became less out-going, more introspective. Each knew the reason for this change, but none uttered it — they were tasting fear and to admit such a thing was not in their nature. Except, of course, for Rhett who had sought to alleviate his apprehension with low-voiced innuendoes directed towards Hedges' bad judgment in getting the troopers into such a position and doubts about his ability to to get them out of it.

But the willingness of the others to listen to the New England fag had grown less as the trek lengthened. Experience had taught them that in a tight corner they could have no better leader than the lean-faced, hooded-eyed Captain. And anyway, in this particular situation, there was no alternative: for, by his dour compliance with every order issued by Hedges, Forrest had proved himself uninclined to challenge for command. No man dared to voice the opinion that the mean-faced sergeant might be as scared as the rest of them. And that when men are scared they look to their strongest ally for leadership.

So the final day on the journey to Richmond passed as quietly as the one before. By turns, one man stood guard at the doorway of the shed while the others slept. Hedges stood his sentry duty from eight until ten and when it was over, he roused all the men. They made a meal of jerked beef, cold beans and plain water, then led their horses outside and mounted.

They rode in silence under a high, bright moon, crossing untracked country until the James River showed up as a silver streak in front of the cluttered skyline of the city. Then they angled on to a turnpike which soon plunged through the buildings of the west side of Richmond. They crossed the river on Mayo's Bridge and saw physical signs of danger as they rode at an easy walk along 14th Street.

Since starting out from the old railroad shed on the spur there had been merely the knowledge that they were within a spit in a high wind of the nerve centre of the Confederacy. Then the silhouette of the city had been just an extension of the shadowy countryside, triggering the imagination into frightening fantasies of evil enemies lurking and watching.

But the many grey uniforms among the civilian garbs visible on the street were no imaginary figments.

"How many men you figure the Reb army has in this town, sir?" Forrest muttered, his eyes flicking suspiciously from left to right.

Hedges was also making a careful surveillance of the street and he reached the conclusion that, barring accidents, they had nothing to fear yet. The street was quite heavily traversed, both by strollers on the sidewalks and riders and vehicles on the pavement. Thus, the Union troopers were not conspicuous as they moved easily through the city, towards the intersection with Broad Street.

"Count the number you can see, then multiply it by any number you think of," Hedges replied. "You might, or might not come close."

"The guys back at Hartford Gap didn't know from nothing, uh?" the sergeant said.

Hedges made the turn on to Broad Street, his mind busy with remembering the relevant details of a map shown to him by the Pinkerton man. "They didn't consider it important," he replied. "We ain't here to take the city. Just kill old man Davis."

Traffic, both riding and walking, was heavier on Broad Street. At the corner of Governor there was a large saloon doing big and noisy business. It was here that Hedges called a halt to the ride, hitching his horse to a rail at the side of the building. A large number of animals were already there.

"I could sure use a drink," Seward said as he hitched his horse and peered in through a window. "Hey, they even got dancing girls in there."

Douglas, Scott and Bell crowded around the youngster to stare through the window. The fact that they had ridden into the very heart of the Confederate capital without being challenged seemed to have injected fresh courage into the men.

Hedges shot a cold glance at Forrest, who gave a curt nod to signal that he, too, recognized this as a bad sign. In the killing business, overconfidence could be a fatal mistake.

Forrest's voice rasped through the din of music and laughter resounding from the big saloon. "You guys?"

The quartet at the window turned away, their eyes still lit with the excitement of the scene through the pane. The mean look on the non-com's face swamped their exhilaration.

"Hell, Frank," Seward said sullenly. "It's been so long since I had me a drink or a woman, I'm starting to feel like a monk."

Forrest jerked a thumb towards the window. "Tough, brother. But you're getting none of that."

Seward shrugged and joined the others in looking towards Hedges.

"Leave the rifles," the Captain ordered. "Only use your side arms if you have to – until after he's dead."

"You got any idea what else we gonna do after he's dead?" Hal Douglas asked, and it was the first spoken doubt in a very long time.

The corporal had a moment of regret that he had voiced it, as he was forced to bow his head under the pressure of a piercing stare from the slitted blue eyes. But then he became aware that the renewal of confidence allowed the others to regard the Captain with quizzical eyes.

"Yeah," Hedges said, just loud enough to be heard above the noise of celebration coming from the saloon. Then he whirled and strode out on to the street.

The troopers watched him for several tense moments, then swung their eyes around to look questioningly at Forrest.

"You reckon he's got an idea, Frank?" John Scott asked.

"Only he knows about that," Forrest replied. "All I know is that I don't."

He led the way out on to the street. Hedges was well advanced along Governor Street and the troopers had to hurry to catch up with him as he entered Capitol Square. It was lit from the surrounding streets and from the windows of the state administration buildings within. Grey uniformed figures with rifles at the slope arms position marched in the pattern of sentry duty at the front, rear and sides of just one building. There were two men covering each approach. But with every sentry making his about-face at a corner, it meant they would all have to be rendered inactive virtually simultaneously to avoid the alarm being raised

The Union infiltrators watched the building from a clump of trees on the north east side of the square. Their presence aroused no suspicion since other people were about — soldiers and civilians, men and women, in couples and groups of three, four or more. It was close to midnight now, but the lateness of the hour did not diminish curiosity about and interest in the home and office of the President of the Confederacy.

"Hard nut to crack," Forrest growled as Hedges finished rolling a cigarette and lit it.

Hedges spat out a flake of tobacco. "Didn't figure it to be easy. But we're hard nut crackers from way back, ain't we?"

"Crackers is right," Rhett drawled.

"How you gonna work it, Captain?" Forrest asked.

"Shortest distance between two points is a straight line," Hedges answered, taking a final drag at the cigarette, then dropping it and grinding out the embers beneath his heel. "Let's try it that way." He glanced at the sergeant, Seward and Douglas. "The four of us first. Bell, Scott and Rhett, give us a twenty yard start, then follow. Move easy, like sightseers. If the going gets rough, every man's on his own.'

He set off before the troopers had a chance to question the tactic, strolling out from among the trees and ambling towards the closed gates in a wrought iron fence surrounding the building. The men he had selected for his group had to take several hurried paces to catch up with him, then slowed to match his casual gait. Other groups and couples were in the area, watching the patrolling sentries and the lighted windows of the building some fifty yards beyond the barrier of the railed fencing.

Hedges halted on the gravel driveway across which the gates were hung and eyed the catch from under the drooping lids. The catch was fastened, but the padlock hung free at the end of a length of chain. Beyond the gates, the driveway cut between neatly trimmed lawns dotted with flower beds and featured both bushes and trees. The bright moon and splashes of light from surrounding streets seemed to broaden the space between gates and building.

The three-strong group of troopers joined the advance party at the gates. They all took their lead from Hedges and stared silently at the building. Some people joined them while others strolled past.

"Forget the quiet way," Hedges hissed at Forrest, the words issuing from the side of his mouth, then leaned close to the sergeant and lowered his voice still further to whisper in his ear.

Forrest grinned. "Make a change for you to take the big risk," he muttered.

"They don't come any bigger than putting my back towards you," Hedges responded softly, then lunged forward.

He burst wide the gates with the heel of his boot and jerked out his Colt as he broke into a run along the arrow-straight driveway. "I'm gonna kill him, the bastard!" he bellowed, firing wildly towards the solid door of the building.

Behind him, pandemonium broke out. The crowd at the gateway shouted in alarm and warning. Those people in other parts of the square yelled demands to know what was happening, then scurried forward to see for themselves when they received no comprehensible answer. Ahead of him, the sentries at the front of the building were going into their about face before the doorway – which meant that those at the sides were midway through their routine and out of sight.

Hedges had covered a quarter of the distance when he fired a second time, taking care to aim. The bullet thudded into the shoulder of one of the surprised sentries and he spun around and crumpled. The second sentry snapped down his rifle, slapping his cheek against the stock.

Forrest drew his Colt and fired from the hip. The bullet whistled close to Hedges' right ear and the Captain cursed the sergeant's narrow miss as he pitched forward, rolled across the skin scraping gravel and came to an untwitching rest on the edge of the lawn.

"I got him!" Forrest yelled above the shouts and grinned into the startled faces of the Union troopers. "I got him! Let's go see him!"

He started forward and the surging of the crowd behind them forced the other troopers to set off in pursuit.

The sentry at the doorway continued to aim his rifle, but he did not squeeze the trigger. The man on the ground struggled into a sitting position and concentrated upon trying to stem the blood oozing from his shoulder wound. Two more sentries appeared at the corners of the building, rifles at the ready. But they held their fire. The door of the building was flung open and four Rebel officers peered anxiously out into the night, revolvers drawn.

"What the hell?" one of them demanded.

Forrest reached the prone form of Hedges first, closely followed by the five other Union men. But within moments a crowd of upwards of fifty excitedly curious bystanders clustered around, and their number was quickly swelled as others ran through the gates to find out the cause of the uproar.

"Let's take him inside where we can see him!" Forrest roared, shoving violently at Billy Seward to indicate the youngster should lift Hedges' feet. The sergeant grasped the Captain's shoulders.

"Halt them!" one of the officers screamed as the crowd surged forward again, led by Forrest and Seward struggling with the burden of Hedges. Rhett, Scott, Bell and Douglas were immediately behind the leaders.

"Over their heads!"

The shout was accompanied by the crack of a pistol shot as the Rebel officer gave an example to the sentries. The men canted their rifles skywards and sent a volley towards the glittering stars. The louder, more insistent crackle of the heavy calibre rifles produced a sharper reaction than the single pistol shot. The vast majority of the crowd halted abruptly.

"Again!"

A second volley silenced the shouts and curtailed the advance of those who had failed to respond to the first. The troopers were out on their own and fully exposed. But the dangerous open area between gate and door had been reduced to ten yards.

"About now, Cap!" Forrest said breathlessly.

Hedges kicked free of Seward's hold on his feet and used his own strength to supplement the shove which Forrest gave him. He hit the ground in a faltering run for a few paces, then corrected it, bringing up the Colt and snapping off a shot. The troopers, strung out in an uneven line of headlong advance, were only a second behind him in firing their guns.

The surprise of seeing an apparently dead man rise and run towards them shocked the Rebel soldiers and officers into a fatal second of numbness. Bullets tore into their bodies and heads and they were flung backwards, splashing great gouts of blood across finely trimmed lawn and flawlessly whitened steps.

The Union men, led by Hedges, leapt across the sprawled bodies in the doorway and lunged into the elegantly furnished hallway of the building, sheering off to right and left as a hail of bullets whistled after them. Then Bell slammed the massive door closed. Civilians and soldiers in the crowd, late in realizing they had unwittingly aided an assault against the Presidential headquarters, sent a futile fusillade of shots towards the door. The wood exploded splinters, but was a solid defence against penetration.

Inside, Hedges wasted no time after raking his slitted eyes over the hallway, brightly lit by a sparkling crystal chandelier. There were five doors leading off at each side and a pair of double doors at the rear, beneath the elegantly curved wings of a flying staircase. He pointed the Colt up towards the ceiling and fired two quick shots, so close together they sounded as one. The fixture holding the chandelier was blasted apart and the entire unit crashed down. Glass shattered and flaming oil streaked across the plush carpet.

As doors were flung open, the troopers leapt across the licking flames and fired their Colts. The Rebels replied with a wild volley. The troopers reached the double doors as a group and Hedges and Forrest lashed out with their boots together. The doors sprang open and crashed back against the walls on either side. The men pulled up short and looked into the face of the man they had come to kill, stern and angular above a high winged collar and topped by an unruly mass of hair swept off the forehead.

But the face was not real. It looked down at them from a portrait hung on the far wall, regarding the intruders along the length of a polished table. There was a vacant chair at the head of the table and a row of similarly empty chairs down each side. The two Gatling guns were mounted on rostrums flanking the head of the table. Each was manned by two gunners. Infantrymen with muskets aimed were ranged along the far wall to each side of the rapid fire guns. The flames roared in the hallway and more soldiers moved towards the rear of the Union troopers through the acrid smoke.

"Outta the frigging fire and down the frigging pan," Forrest muttered sourly as Hedges dropped his Colt.

"You ready to tell us your idea now?" Douglas snarled as he joined the others in releasing his gun.

"Don't knock it 'til you know it," Hedges replied easily.

He, like the others, jerked forward slightly as revolver muzzles were jabbed into their backs. None of the Rebels had uttered a word. The abrupt hiss of steam told of attempts to extinguish the flames.

"You can come in now, sir!" a young Lieutenant called, coming away from the wall and grinning meanly towards the prisoners.

A door at one side of the long, narrow room opened and a grey haired man with general's insignia on his uniform arms stepped through and to the right. President Jefferson Davis moved through the doorway. Hedges thought the man taller and thinner than he had expected. A wry smile played at the corners of his mouth and lit his eyes, exhibiting a humour at which the portrait gave no clue.

"Did you really think we would have no contingency plan in the event you evaded capture and reached me?" he asked, his eyes moving over the faces of the Union troopers and settling on the lean features of Hedges.

"We had to give it the old college try," the Union Captain replied.

Jefferson Davis inclined his head and moved to sit in the chair at the head of the table, flanked by the evil snouts of the Gatling guns. The hissing ceased and the final traces of smoke drifted. "I'm obliged to you," the Rebel President said. "That incident at the theatre was very dramatic. It gave me an idea."

"I hope it's better than yours!" Forrest rasped, close to Hedges' ear.

"Lock up the prisoners, general," Davis ordered, his expression thoughtful. "Yes, a fine idea," he said softy, then raised his voice. "And find out if that actor fellow Booth is still in the city."

"What's he mean?" Bell asked as the Union troopers were urged to turn and then marched across the fire-blackened hallway.

Hedges shrugged. "Another theatre of operations. Guess it means curtains for somebody."

The thin man and Howard Gold had their horses in the barn. Edge held a gun on the men as they saddled the animals then all three walked their horses well clear of the house before mounting. The half-breed rode behind them, Winchester pointing between them and ready to flick to left or right at the first hint of trouble.

They rode up to the wide pass, keeping the pace slow and easy to avoid the possibility of stampeding the great herd of cattle grazing all around them. Through the pass was a rocky plateau traversed by a well-trodden trail over which countless steers had been driven. A column of rock, pointing skywards like a crooked finger, marked the start of a spur trail that swung to the north. This was the way the trio went. The ground began to slope downwards, rock giving way to soil upon which grass, brush and some trees grew. But there was never enough shade from the moonlight to allow the captives an opportunity to jump their captor.

"How many times you pull this stunt before?" Edge asked after a silence of more than three miles.

"Five," the thin man replied, and turned in the saddle, his face anxious. "Nobody ever got hurt. And this is the last time. We've got enough money now."

"For Jefferson to give the girl the kind of life her old man did?"

The thin man nodded. "That's right. Dave's my nephew. Howard here is Julia's brother. The boys who pulled the hold-up are my sons. Everybody who knows Dave and Julia reckon they're made for each other. Except for Matt Gold. He measures a man by his wealth."

Edge spat. "Pretty soon he ought to consider me as really something, uh?"

The thin man swallowed hard and turned to face front again. Thirty minutes later they reached the head of a valley that was almost identical to the one in which Matthew Gold's ranch was sited. The same lush pasture with roughly the same size of herd grazing it. Even the same sort of house and outbuildings – when they were finished. At present there was just the skeleton framework of timber uprights and cross beams, waiting for the huge pile of planks stacked to one side to be nailed into position to form walls and roofs

The buckboard, with the horse no longer in the shafts, was parked outside a large tent, glowing with lamplight from inside. Jefferson and the girl heard the approach of the horsemen and stepped out through the flap. They looked along the trail with expectant smiles, which did not fade until the three men came within the aura of the lamplight. Then they saw the empty holsters of the thin man and Howard Gold and realized the significance of the apparently casually held Winchester in Edge's hands.

"What's happened?" Jefferson demanded as the thin man and Gold slid from their saddles. Julia gasped, her eyes wide in recognition. "You know him?" her fiance snapped

The girl couldn't talk around the lump in her throat.

Edge curled back his thin lips. "Guess you might say I know her pretty well," he drawled. "From the bottom up."

Julia winced at the memory, made a move to reach for her rump, then stayed her hand and coloured.

"He wants his money," the thin man explained, then looked directly at Julia, his expression melancholy. "He made a large bet and he won. His due is twenty-two thousand."

The girl gasped again. "We've just finished counting it. There's only five thousand."

The thin man's expression did not change, as if he already knew what the take was. As stakeholder, he probably did.

"It's to furnish the house," Jefferson said.

Edge trained the Winchester on him. "Go into the tent and bring out the money, lady," he instructed coldly, hooded eyes glinting in the lamplight. "You bring out anything else and your next trip to church will be for a funeral instead of a wedding."

Jefferson seemed about to countermand the order, but the

killer glint warned him to remain silent. The girl whirled and ducked into the tent. It took her less than thirty seconds to put the money back in the bag and bring the bag outside. She strode purposefully towards the half-breed and thrust the bag at him. He nestled the stock of the Winchester under his armpit as he accepted the burden and hung it over the saddle horn. Julia backed away to stand beside Jefferson.

"You guys pointed guns at me and made the mistake of not using them," the half-breed said to the thin man and Howard Gold. "But you get to live because I'm still owed. Five grand off of twenty-two leaves seventeen." He raked the rifle back and forth along the row of tense faces. "Be quicker if four of you work at raising the balance."

"There'll be six of us," Julia corrected miserably.

Edge shook his head. "Four."

The thin man's face was transformed into a mask of anguish. "You mean . . . ?"

"Somebody got hurt," Edge confirmed. "Two bodies, matter of fact."

"You bastard!" the thin man exploded, and made to lunge forward. But both Jefferson and Gold laid restraining hands on him.

"But I got my good points," Edge said easily, jerking the reins to wheel the gelding. "I'm lending you seventeen grand until the next time I'm through this part of the country."

"Big deal!" Gold spat. His tone became sardonic. "You want to tell us your name so we can make out a marker?"

Edge looked over his shoulder at the quartet standing before the lighted tent amid the half completed ranch-house. "No marker needed, feller. I know what I'm owed and who owes it me."

"I'd like to know your name," Julia said hoarsely. "So if I ever see it on a gravestone I can spit on it."

Edge showed her his cold grin and thudded in his heels to lunge the gelding into a gallop. His voice drifted back across the thunder of hooves: "You folks can just call me the loan arranger!"